TARGET ME

AT ALL COSTS SERIES
BOOK ONE

TL HAMILTON

AUTHOR'S NOTE

Target Me contains themes that may be triggering to some readers. Please use caution when reading.

Triggering themes include, but are not limited to:

Suicide

Assault

Consensual D/s dynamics

Spanking

Breath play

Drugging

This story is a work of fiction and should not be used as a guide for any sexual activities. If you wish to experiment with kink, please do your research with reputable resources.

This story was previously published in the "Tease Me" anthology 2023

If I haven't scared you off yet, HAPPY READING!!

PROLOGUE

Logan

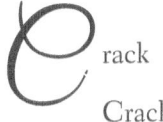rack

Crack

Crack

The three-volley salute echoed through the trees, bouncing off gravestones set in neat lines like pearly white teeth, sprouting from verdant green, well-maintained grass. American flags waved in greeting to the newest resident of the cemetery. One who shouldn't be here. None of us should have been. My skin crawled beneath my uniform as the sun ducked behind a cloud, as though even that flaming orb wanted nothing to do with the distraught sobbing I was doing my damndest to tune out.

Losing someone in wartime was one thing. In the heat of battle, every one of us was willing to put our lives on the line for God and country. But sometimes the real battle happened after the guns fell silent.

When there was nothing tangible to fight, there were nights when the brain cannibalized itself. When the screaming in your head got so loud that alcohol, drugs, sex, whatever poison you chose, was the only thing that would drown it out.

For some people, those things didn't work well enough, and when death was your business... Well... there was a lot that didn't seem so scary when you'd become desensitized to it.

Across the way, dressed in a black pantsuit and gripping the triangular shape of the star-spangled banner she'd been ceremonially presented, Charlie was pale as a ghost. Tears streaked her cheeks, and she flinched when someone behind her grasped her shoulder. Too young to be a widow, she looked lost amongst the group of mourners surrounding her.

Shifting subtly, I dropped my gaze away from the casket as it was lowered into the earth, away from the final resting place of my brother-in-arms, and focused on a dirty teddy bear that lay facedown beside a bunch of rotting flowers on a headstone inches from my highly polished shoe. *Grace Everly*, the headstone read. 2014 - 2023. Fuck. Fate was a bitch.

I threw up a salute as "Taps" was played. The bugle just barely loud enough to drown out Damon's moans behind me.

I couldn't imagine losing a brother, let alone a twin, and the guys and I had been taking turns checking in on Damon and Charlie since the news of Adrien's suicide had broken.

Damon was dealing with it about as well as could be expected; lots of drinking, swearing, and crying.

As the other attendees moved away from the grave, I reached down and righted the teddy bear, resting his back against the stone so he could be Grace's eyes and guard her against threats.

A heavy hand landed on my shoulder, startling me more than I cared to admit.

"Lost in your thoughts, Tanner?" The deep bass cut through me as it always did, loosening my muscles and clearing my head in the way only my mentor could.

"Good to see you, General." I grinned, offering a hand in greeting. He knocked it aside in favor of pulling me in for a brief hug.

General Walker had always carried himself with a charisma that demanded the best from his men. His quick wit and wicked tactical mind inspired loyalty that was hard to find in other parts of the military. I was the lucky son of a bitch he had chosen to take on straight out of training, and under his leadership, I rose through the ranks until I was the one looking for a protégé.

Life, however, had other plans.

"Not a general anymore, son. Then again, a bird told me you're hanging up the uniform, too."

I grimaced. Explaining my reasons for leaving the forces hadn't been on my dance card today. I was here to grieve a peer and hopefully keep the guy's brother from following him into an early grave.

"How are you finding politics, Sir? Treating you well?" I asked, redirecting the conversation.

Walker snorted. "It's more of a cesspool than what we saw on deployment. Never trust a politician, boy. They're dirtier than worms and just as slippery."

"You ruffling feathers already?" I joked, nodding absently to the chaplain as he made his way past, Bible tucked under one arm.

"Somethin' like that. It's still easier than dealing with Avery sometimes. Never have daughters, my boy. You can divorce a wife, but daughters will bleed you dry until the day you foist them off on another poor soul."

I offered a commiserating smile. "No chance of that happening. I'm not planning on settling down. Not ever, if I can help it."

"Smart lad." General Walker slapped my shoulder again as we wandered toward the road where cars lined the gutter as neatly as the graves behind us.

"If you ever want to get into personal security, or something of the sort, I have a lot of friends willing to pay an obscene amount of money to protect their interests. Think about it. Easy money, and if you're lucky, you'll still get to shoot someone occasionally."

I hadn't thought much about what I would do after my last day in the military, but the idea of acting as hired muscle for some pompous socialite who probably knew nothing of the real world turned me cold. I didn't have the patience for other people like Walker did. God knew, I'd probably knock out the person I was supposed to be protecting to make them shut up if I was in a bad enough mood. Nope, I was better off finding somewhere to work with my hands.

In the classifieds that morning, I'd come across a farmhouse for sale. Even in the picture, I could tell the roof was sagging, and I could only guess how much work it would need. In the middle of a graveyard, confronted with the question of "what next", I decided I would buy the house. Renovate the shit out of it and maybe build a hobby farm or something. Idle hands were supposed to be the devil's playground and all, so the project would do me good.

"Thank you, sir, but I don't think I'm cut out for protection detail."

He grunted, his face set in an expression I'd seen too many times to trust. This wasn't the last I'd hear of it, and the thought was as frustrating as it was comforting.

"It's your fucking fault! He didn't kill himself. I know he didn't—"

The General and I spun in unison, acting like the well-trained soldiers we were as we reached for weapons we wouldn't find on our ceremonial garb. The disturbance had caused many of the funeral attendees to pause in the process of entering their cars to gawk at the spectacle that had been building since we arrived.

Damon was frantic, lunging against the hold Bear had around his middle and cursing out anyone who got too close. His bloodshot eyes rolled in his head, his tie was loose, and buttons were already missing from his shirt. His breath huffed audibly through his nose as Bear slapped a meaty palm over his mouth.

"Come on, man. Don't be like this. Adrien wouldn't want this. Look. Charlie can hear you. She doesn't need this shit today. You lost your brother, but she lost her husband, too."

"I'd better go help with that," I muttered apologetically.

General Walker nodded and moved off toward a shiny black SUV that screamed future president, while I turned back to my drunken, grief-stricken friend.

"Hey, man, let's get in my car, and I'll take you home to bed." Bear maneuvered Damon into the backseat of my truck and strapped him in before climbing into the passenger side. As we pulled away from the cemetery, Damon seemed to run out of steam, sagging in his skin. It made him appear older than his twenty-eight years.

"They fucking killed him," he muttered, so quietly I could barely hear him over the engine. I tossed a glance at Bear, who shrugged and checked the rearview to find Damon already passed out. Safe in the company of his brothers-in-arms.

1

AVERY

S omething wasn't right.

The thought occurred to me as I dropped my load of shopping bags inside the front door. More and more over the past week, I'd developed this paranoia. This feeling, like my every move was under constant surveillance. In the middle of a crowded mall, I found myself cataloging faces, wondering if the man with a baseball cap had been in the previous store with me. If the woman in the business suit was watching me when I wasn't looking.

Being home alone was the worst. The sprawling property my father had insisted on buying was beautiful during the day. An entertainer's paradise where men with big wallets could flaunt their wealth in a dick-measuring competition that I would rather have avoided if my role weren't always to play hostess.

Since my mother had made it out, I had taken over the role of *woman of the house*, and I often wondered if I could be free too if only I had the courage to be less than the perfect version of a daughter my father wanted to show the world.

Yes, by day the property was lovely.

At night, the trees seemed to hum with ominous energy, as though thousands of eyes shone from the shadows in waiting. For what? I didn't know, but I'd taken to drawing the curtains before sunset, like they could shield me from the things that go bump in the night.

"Father? Are you home?" I called, moving into the kitchen. A pile of mail sat in the center of the clean counter, and beside it, a perfectly penned note informing me my father would be gone for the next three days. Not a great surprise. He was due to hit the campaign trail at the beginning of next month and had increasingly chosen to stay in the city, which I would usually love. Not so much when it left me in an empty house while I was feeling like this.

Shaking off the sense of unease, I pulled a pre-cut serving of lasagna from the refrigerator, silently blessing Luciana for leaving a decent-sized portion for me. Her cooking was second to none, and the reminder that I could enjoy it without my father's disapproving gaze went a long way toward comforting me.

Setting the microwave to work its magic, I distracted myself by shuffling through the envelopes littering the counter. Two were addressed to my father, one was a bill, junk mail, junk mail, junk mail... The last envelope was blank. Heavy.

Frowning, I pushed the discarded mail aside and leaned my elbows on the counter, wondering if I should have left it for my father. After a moment of contemplation, I tore it open and flinched at the sound of metal hitting the granite countertop.

"What...?"

A key glinted up at me. One that looked suspiciously like the one I had just used to open the front door. Digging into the ripped envelope, I found a small slip of paper that read "watch your back" in black sharpie.

I glanced around. The kitchen felt larger and more ominous than before.

"It's probably a prank," I muttered, even as I crossed to the French doors that led out to the patio and pulled the curtains across.

A flash of movement made me pause just before I closed the gap completely, but a prolonged survey of the outdoor furniture, rolling lawn, and tree line showed all was still. With a decisive tug, I cut off the view of the yard and almost jumped out of my skin at the loud rattling that announced an incoming call on my cell.

The phone fell silent as I reached for my purse but immediately started up again. Someone wanted to speak to me, not my voicemail. A moment later, my hand came across the jiggling device, and I caught a glimpse of my father's name as I connected the call.

"Where the hell are you?"

"Hello to you too, Dad. Just got your note. You could have just texted, you know?"

"Don't screw around, Avery. Where are you? Are you at home?"

I sighed, checking the microwave to see how long it had left. "Yes, I'm at home. I got in about five minutes ago. What's going on?"

My phone beeped with an incoming text.

"Check your phone, and please tell me one of your idiot friends decided to pull a prank."

"I have no *idiot friends*," I groused, putting the cell on speaker so I could check my messages.

The photo looked like it had been taken at a distance, with a long lens or something. A glass door with beige curtains pulled halfway closed. In the center stood a blonde girl in a red tank top, denim shorts, and...

I looked down at my white Volleys as the room spun for a moment. Someone had taken this picture less than a minute ago and sent it to my father.

"When...?" My tongue felt thick. My lips numb. The key and the note, I was ready to shrug off, but the photo? Why had they sent it to my dad?

"I'm taking this threat seriously." His voice was a deep growl, accompanied by the shuffling sounds of paper.

"What does that mean?" I asked, a stupid, childish hope flaring to life as images of him canceling his campaign to prioritize his family, or even asking me to come on the trail with him, danced through my head.

"It means you're on lockdown until I can get you a babysitter. Do not leave the house. Clearly, someone has decided to sabotage my campaign by compromising you. Let me make this clear. You will not be the reason I lose this election, so sit your ass down, stay indoors, and behave for whoever I send to look after you. Am I clear?"

"Yes, Sir," I muttered, momentarily distracted by the beeping of the microwave announcing my meal was ready.

"Wait, who are you planning on sending?"

When there was no response, I pulled the cell away from my ear. He'd ended the call.

"Love you too, Dad. Asshole."

A cheery beep reminded me of my hot meal, but my stomach turned at the thought.

My dad hated me. I was getting a babysitter—I was twenty-five, for Christ's sake—and apparently, I had a stalker... or something. Things were complicated, to say the least.

Shuffling toward the front entryway, I folded the empty shopping bags I had brought in and paused. Shit. A babysitter was really going to complicate things for me.

There were parts of my life my dad wouldn't approve of. Things that I did just for me that I had no intention of giving up. Luckily, I was resourceful. Whoever he found to watch over me would just have to come around to my way of thinking.

THE DEEP TOLL OF OUR PRETENTIOUS DOORBELL pulled me from a deep sleep the next morning. Groaning, I slapped around on my bedside table until I found my cell. Six a.m. What the hell was wrong with whoever was coming to call at that ungodly hour? When the bell tolled a second and third time, it became apparent that whoever it was, they weren't planning on waiting to visit at a more reasonable time of day.

Ding dong.

I almost screamed as the thing sounded *a fourth time* and hauled myself out of bed, ready to bite the head off the early morning visitor.

My bare feet slapped against the tiled floor of the entryway, and I was in a full fury by the time I reached for the door handle.

"What?" I growled, yanking the door open.

A black t-shirt stretched tight over a crazy-wide chest sat at eye level as I spat my admittedly rude, but totally justifiable, non-greeting. Squinting against the glare of the barely risen, early morning sun, I kept the scowl on my face even as I perused the square-cut, clean-shaven jaw and surprisingly plump lips. Aviator sunglasses reflected my unkempt appearance, and it took a conscious effort not to smooth my hair down as I noticed he was wearing a scowl to match my own underneath the peak of a black ball cap.

His head dropped in his own blatant assessment, reminding me I wore nothing but a near see-through white tank and booty shorts. Ugh. Crossing my arms over my chest— because even if he did wake me up, I had more decorum than to let some stranger ogle my nips—I leaned against the doorframe and cocked a brow.

"Can I help you?"

"I'm reporting for babysitting duty. You going to let me in?" His voice was deep and full of gravel, like liquor and campfire smoke, and I mostly kept the shudder of pleasure to myself at hearing the words roll off his tongue.

"Depends," I said, forcing a smirk onto my face.

I was developing a suspicion of who this might be, and if I was right, making his life hell was going to be my new favorite pastime.

In my father's forty-year military career, he'd had many men work under him, but in the last five years, only one name had been brought up again and again. A man of "perfect repute," who graduated basic training with honors and completed his bachelor a year ahead of schedule. He was the man my father thought of as a son.

"Logan Tanner," he said, touching surprisingly well-manicured fingertips to his forehead in an approximation of a salute.

I hummed, pretending to think things through. "How do I know I'm not letting the fox into the henhouse? You could be anyone. I'd hate to make a mistake like that."

"Stop playing games, little girl," he growled, scooping up a khaki duffle from by his feet and stepping past me into the house.

Damn. He smelled like leather and bourbon, with a hint of fresh-cut wood, which made me wonder what he had been doing before he decided to invade my space.

"I don't need a babysitter."

I trailed him from the entrance hall into the open plan living area, ignoring the way he looked around the space as though impressed by the surroundings. It was a façade. A nicely presented ruse designed to impress and intimidate while making the owner seem more influential than he was. *Fake it until you make it* was more than my dad's slogan; it was his goddamn way of life.

"Your father thinks otherwise, and until my orders change, you can consider me your shadow. You're welcome, hen." He still hadn't removed his sunglasses, keeping his eyes hidden, but his teeth were perfectly straight and white as he flashed a nasty smile at me which was more wolf than fox.

Game on.

2

LOGAN

*T*he call had come through around midnight.

"Tanner. I need a favor."

I brushed wood shavings off the lathe I'd silenced to answer the call as General Walker explained the developing situation.

"She's a high-value target and a complication I don't need with the work I'm doing. I need someone I trust to keep her in line. I'll pay well, of course. I'd consider you a private contractor."

I'd agreed because... why the hell not? I owed so much to the man, and even though the idea of being someone's private security guard still left me cold, I would do it. For him.

The call didn't last much longer after I agreed. The General knew better than to give me time to reconsider, especially after the years I'd spent listening to him lament his difficult daughter. Other than what the General had told me, Avery

Walker was an enigma to me. The few times I'd been invited to the General's house, I'd declined. The idea of schmoozing politicians and high-ranking officials was about as appealing as... well... babysitting a grown woman who was spoiled and completely naïve about the world.

Shit.

Woodworking hadn't seemed like enough of a distraction after the conversation I'd just had, so I took a moment to pack up my supplies and changed into a tank top and basketball shorts, then hit the road for a run.

There had always been something exhilarating about midnight running. While the world slept, I pounded out the miles along dirt roads and pavement. My shoes slapped a rhythm that worked me into a trance-like state, restoring my mind while, paradoxically, exhausting my body.

The routine was familiar, something I grabbed on to when the nightmares tore at my grip on reality. One foot in front of the other. One day at a time. The concept of breaking life into bite-sized pieces when it became overwhelming was something I had learned from an AA meeting I'd forced Adrien to attend.

We'd sat in the back, tepid coffee in hand, while Adrien watched the exit. We hadn't even left the building before he suggested a trip to the liquor store on the way home. Needless to say, my efforts hadn't helped him much, but they had helped me in a small way. Control what you can, leave the rest. The serenity prayer was a good idea... Shame I had no hope for it.

Peace was a foreign concept to soldiers.

Five miles out from the shithole I'd decided to move into before even starting renovations, I slowed to a stop outside the twenty-four-hour gym I frequented at all hours of the day or night. Scanning the entry fob, I waved at the camera that served as staff during night hours and took a moment to enjoy the whole lot of no one here that came with an insomniac's workout schedule.

For two hours, I pushed my body through a grueling mix of upper body weights and functional training exercises, until my muscles screamed in protest, my heart thundering in my ears. I drank deeply from the water fountain, wiped down the equipment I'd used, then set out for the five-mile run home.

On the grass out the front of the ranch, I ran through the yoga exercises the physiotherapist had given me for a back injury that never should have happened before heading inside for a shower.

The warm water sluiced over my body, rinsing away the sweat and grime of my workout until it was as though it had never happened. There one minute, gone the next, and only what lay beneath the surface left behind to tell the tale. I shook my head hard, beads of water splashing against the cheap plastic curtain I'd bought to keep the bathroom from flooding, and turned my thoughts to my new assignment.

What I needed was a plan. Every successful mission in history came down to carefully laid and executed plans. Avery was the assignment. No, not Avery. Miss. Walker. I couldn't get overly familiar with an assignment. Remaining objective would be mission critical. Protect the girl, find the threat, and eradicate it. Simple. Easy. I'd be back to reframing my new house in no time.

A heavy clunk echoed through the wall a second before the stream above me dropped to below freezing. I cursed, turning off the water with a flick of the tap, then cursed again as a faint hissing confirmed I had a leak in the hot water line. Wrapping a towel around my hips, I stomped outside and turned the water off at the main.

The sky was a deep purple, the softest hint of light promising the start of a new day.

"No time like the present," I decided, wandering inside and pulling a pair of jeans out of my kit bag to cover my ass. Next came a black t-shirt and ball cap to complete the *I'm here to do a job, don't fuck with me* vibe.

As I grabbed the keys to my truck, a niggle in my hamstring reminded me protein would be a good idea at some point. Instead, I picked two bananas out of the fruit bowl I'd set up and ate them in three bites a piece as I backed out of my driveway and headed for an area code that was far more upscale than the one I left in my dust.

My breath escaped through my teeth in a whistle of appreciation as I double checked the address and confirmed the monster house in front of me was exactly where I was supposed to be. I wondered how the General had come to live there. Maybe his ex-wife had insisted on it. Or the daughter. Either way, I wasn't looking forward to staying in the place for longer than necessary, and that was before I considered how much more difficult it would be to secure such a large premises.

One step at a time. I could assess current security protocols once I had met the assignment. With a final steadying breath, I pulled myself out of my truck, grabbing my pack and ignoring the cramping in my legs from the lactic acid buildup. I knew better than to sit in my truck so soon after a big workout, but nothing for it. I'd walk it out.

Huge marble columns bracketed the front door, the slippery stone spilling down the front stairs in a way that made me wonder if I shouldn't watch my step. Beside the heavy-looking wooden door was a brass doorbell that could have been antique or just really well designed. A booming chime broke out as I pushed the bell, and I stood back, dropping my pack by my feet. The sound faded, and seeing as it had elicited no response, I put it to work again a few more times. Eventually, the slapping of footsteps preceded the arrival of what I could only describe as an angry pixie.

"What?" she growled, throwing open the door.

Her attitude faltered as she caught sight of me, and I carefully hid a smirk as her eyes burned a path over my body. I couldn't blame her. I was doing the same thing. White-blonde hair stood out from her head in a mess that could conservatively be called a bird's nest. I wondered if a blue jay might fly out if we waited long enough. Fierce hazel eyes narrowed, and it occurred to me she looked nothing like her father until she pulled that exact expression.

"Can I help you?" she asked, crossing her arms over full breasts I had tried and failed not to notice. I was a man, for fuck's sake, and her body was worth looking at, even if it was completely off limits.

"I'm reporting for babysitting duty. You going to let me in?"

"Depends."

Shit, she was throwing me off my game. She had someone following her, and here I was, wanting to be let in with no introduction.

"Logan Tanner," I said, touching my brow in a small salute in hopes I could turn the conversation around.

She hummed, a coy look passing over her face that made me bristle before she opened her pretty pink mouth again.

"How do I know I'm not letting the fox into the henhouse? You could be anyone. I'd hate to make a mistake like that."

Her words were logical. Her tone of voice was bratty and immediately triggered a response in me that was entirely inappropriate for the situation. I wanted to punish her. Bind those long, toned legs and turn her ass the same color as the nipples I could see peeking through the fabric of her shirt.

Fuck this.

"Stop playing games, little girl."

I scooped up my belongings, pushing past my charge into the house and ignoring her protest in favor of perusing the interior. Large open spaces, lots of windows. No cameras on the inside—I'd have to change that. I wondered whether a property this big had a dedicated security room or just an app. I'd have to check with the General.

"I don't need a babysitter."

She was fucking pouting. My hand twitched with the need to spank her, but, being the professional I was, I reminded her exactly why I was here.

"Your father thinks otherwise, and until my orders change, you can consider me your shadow. You're welcome, hen." I grinned, proud of the callback to her previous metaphor, and decided that would be her codename from here on out.

Hen. I could see from her face she hated it already. Perfect.

"Are you going to show me around?"

She grunted and headed for the staircase, the curve of her ass appearing and disappearing in tantalizing glimpses I should have turned away from.

"Is that a yes?" I asked, trying to focus on the task at hand.

"It's a do *whatever you want*. I'm going back to bed until a more decent hour."

"It's practically lunchtime," I called after her, barely able to suppress a chuckle at the middle finger she flipped over her shoulder.

The slam of a door upstairs caused the smile to slip from my face as I shifted into work mode. I couldn't forget why I was here. Someone was threatening the General through his daughter, and I wasn't going to let them get away with it. Shit. As fun as it was to needle the girl, I couldn't forget that not only was she an assignment, she was also the daughter of someone I respected immensely.

Priorities straightened once more, I took my time walking the property, probing weak points in the fence line, and devising plans to strengthen the perimeter. I plotted points around the first floor to recommend camera installation and wondered if contact sensors on the windows would be overkill.

I made notes of all my suggestions and sent them in a preliminary report to the General before wandering into the kitchen in search of coffee.

The machine had finished dumping liquid gold into my mug when Avery came flying down the stairs, scraping her hair into a ponytail with a hair elastic in her teeth.

"I'm late. Shit, I'm really late."

"Late for what?" I asked, eyeing her black yoga pants and t-shirt curiously. Her tennis shoes squeaked on the floorboards, she pulled up so quickly, and she eyed me cautiously, securing her hair in place.

"Shopping. I'm... late for shopping. Don't worry about it. I'll be back in two hours."

The click of a lock was loud in the silence that followed her statement. Moving in a way that was second nature, I pulled the nine millimeter I'd stashed in the waistband of my jeans and pointed it calmly at the front hall where the tap of shoes announced the arrival of an unannounced visitor.

"Wait—" Avery started.

A shadow preceded the visitor, and I cocked my weapon, moving in quickly to aim at the head—

Of a small dark-haired woman who took one look at the weapon pointed in her face and slapped it away. A stream of Portuguese that finished with, "Devia fazê-lo, seu filho da mãe estúpido!"

"My Portuguese is a little rusty, but I think she just called me a stupid son of a bitch," I muttered, staring in wonder at the tiny woman who moved straight past me and into the kitchen, clucking her tongue at the mess I'd made of the coffee maker.

"You missed the part where she threatened to shoot you?" Avery asked, cocking an eyebrow as she edged toward the door I was blocking.

"Hold up, give me a second, and I'll come with you."

"Oh, you don't have to do that. I'll just be browsing shoes. Very boring." Her eyes shifted toward the door, body practically vibrating with the need to leave.

"You've already forgotten the part where I said I'd be your shadow for the foreseeable future?" I asked, retrieving my ball cap and sunglasses from the kitchen bench and downing my coffee, not trusting her to wait if given the chance.

"I'm going to be buying lingerie. I don't feel comfortable having you there. We only just met. Seriously, I won't tell if you don't. I've been to the mall plenty of times. I promise it's safe."

"No deal," I said, grabbing the keys to my truck and steering her out the door. "I'll wait outside the store if you'll feel more comfortable, but you aren't going alone."

Avery climbed into the passenger seat with a huff. This girl was clearly not used to the word no. I suppressed the urge to teach her a lesson and slid into the driver's side, starting the engine and waiting for directions.

3

AVERY

Shit. The guy had pulled a gun on Luciana. It should not have turned me on as much as it did. The way his face had darkened, going from curious to dangerous in a heartbeat, was going to feature in late night fantasies for a while to come. Who was I kidding? Even without that encounter, I knew Captain Tanner's crazy hot body would be starring in my dreams.

His large hands tightened on the steering wheel. They would be strong, but would they be rough? Or smooth? Rough. I decided, watching with far too much interest as he downshifted to take the corner smoothly. He was a good driver. I didn't know if that was an attractive feature or not.

Ugh. I knew better than to find Army guys attractive. They were never worth the hype, anyway. The clicking of his turn signal reminded me I had more pressing issues to worry about. I needed to lose my personal guard for a while.

"You can let me out here and just come back in two hours. Deal? Great," I babbled, unclicking my seatbelt and reaching for the handle.

Logan grunted, reaching across and pinning me in place. The move brought us face to face, and his chest pressed against my breasts in a way that made my heart race. Heat crawled up my neck as his breath tickled across my lips. Without thinking, I lifted my chin.

He pulled back, securing the seatbelt across my body again with a smirk that said he knew exactly what he was doing to me.

"Not a chance in hell. Stay buckled up until I get us parked. I'm sure the shoes will wait for you."

Asshole.

I glanced at the clock, cringing as the time ticked over the hour. I was officially late. I had to lose the guy as quickly as possible.

Logan swung into a parking space, and I was out of the car before he had finished applying the parking brake.

"Hey, wait up," he shouted, scrambling out of his truck and pausing for a second to ensure the central locking engaged before jogging after me.

"Seriously, what's the rush?"

"None of your business," I said, moving faster and mentally cursing his long legs as he kept up effortlessly.

"You aren't going to outrun me, hen, so you may as well get used to me."

We'll see about that.

I turned into the first lingerie store I found and breathed a sigh of relief as he halted at the entrance, as promised. My backup plan had been buying tampons. That would have taken more finesse, because he would likely have waited at the top of the aisle. Sliding into the changing area out back, I looked around, hoping for a loading dock, an emergency exit, anything that would help get me out of the mall and into the building I actually needed to go to.

"Can I help you?" The sales assistant was a couple of years younger than me. Raven black hair and cat-eye glasses added a pinup vibe to the woman who could make or break my escape plan.

"Um. Is there a restroom around here anywhere? It's kind of an emergency," I whispered conspiratorially.

The girl's face transformed from suspicion to empathy in a heartbeat.

"Not in here, but take that door, and there's one halfway down the alley. There's a padlock on it, but no one ever bothers to lock it during the day."

I thanked her profusely, moving around the stack of boxes that hid the door I needed. Peeking back into the shop, I could see Logan's large frame looming near the entrance. Still where I left him. Thank God. With more confidence, I slipped outside and ran the perimeter of the mall to a building sitting on the corner of the next block. A converted warehouse, it was easy to miss if you didn't know the signage.

I pushed through the door and bowed low, straightening to grin at the people inside.

"Sorry I'm late."

&

Two hours later, I was in a much better mood as I entered the mall. I wondered if Logan was where I left him. I'd decided to tell him I got locked outside after going to the restroom or something of the sort. It was close enough to the truth for him to buy, surely.

The mall was relatively quiet, unsurprising, given it was two-thirty in the afternoon on a weekday. Generally, the lunch rush lasted from eleven to two when the nearby worksites took a lunch break. I could have set my watch by the peaks and flows of the mall patronage, the only time it differed was around holidays when people took longer lunches hoping to get ahead on their shopping before the mall became an all-out battlefield on Christmas Eve.

I passed the neon pink sign of the store I had escaped out of two hours before and noticed a distinct absence of tall, dark, and protective. Maybe he'd decided to wait in the food court?

There were several 'husband chairs' scattered around the mall, and I imagined for a moment coming across his large frame squeezed into one of the lounges. Could see him checking his watch and sighing in the long-suffering way I had seen so many men do when their wives were absorbed by the lights and sales the mall had to offer.

Before I could find Logan, someone found me.

The heavy body hit me from the side, the weight behind them driving me into the shadows of a service corridor. Instinct took over and, moving with the force of the body, I threw off their balance, aiming a well-placed kick at their crotch and pulling my knee a second before I broke their nose.

"What the hell, man?" I shrieked as Logan doubled over, breathing deeply but not releasing the tight grip on my arm.

His fingers tightened to the point of bruising, and I squirmed in his grip as he continued to breathe through the injury I'd just inflicted on him. Sorry, not sorry. He should have said my name or something like a normal person.

After a moment more of just breathing, he straightened and gripped my other arm, holding me at arm's length with a thunderous look on his face.

"Where the fuck have you been?"

"Shopping."

"Bullshit."

"I got locked outside—"

"Bullshit."

"I just—"

"Bullshit."

Any shred of remorse I might have felt was waning at a rapid rate as I considered just kicking him in the balls a second time.

"Are you going to let me talk?"

"No."

Screw this.

I raised my knee, ready to kick again, and Logan flattened his body against mine, holding me in place with his hips and effectively removing the range of movement needed to hurt him. Bastard.

"I'm rather fond of my dick. If you even think about kicking it again, you'll be kissing it better."

"Promise?" The word was out of my mouth before I could call it back, but it had the desired effect. His eyes heated before he blinked and backed up.

"Stop changing the subject. Where. Were. You?"

I sighed and, rather than answering, started off in the direction of his truck.

"Avery."

My feet stumbled over the next step, but I resolutely kept moving. I was done here, and despite what he thought, I owed him nothing. He was an agent for my father.

Nothing more.

It didn't take long for him to catch me, but at least he stopped demanding answers. The drive home was a lot more tense than the drive out, weighed down by words unspoken and resentments that belonged to others not present.

As soon as we reached the house, I took off, hiding myself away in my attic sanctuary while Logan stomped around doing God knew what downstairs.

Eventually, hunger and the need to shower drove me downstairs, and after satisfying the latter, I wandered into the kitchen as the setting sun barged through the French doors in an obnoxiously blinding display that made me wish I'd stayed upstairs. Tying my wet hair up into a messy bun to keep it out of the way, I went into the fridge to find two plates of chickpea curry ready to heat.

"Bless you, Luciana," I muttered, sliding one of the dishes into the microwave to heat.

When I was younger, Luciana had made it her mission to teach me to cook. To this day, we joked that I was her kryptonite. Her one impossible challenge. I had curdled scrambled eggs, repeatedly burned toast, and after we had to call the fire department during an unfortunate venture into cooking rice, we had decided it was better for everyone involved if I didn't try to do anything more than make coffee or microwave pre-prepared food in the kitchen.

Perching on a stool to wait, I looked around the lower level, wondering where Logan had gone. Maybe I'd managed to scare him off already. The thought was funny until I looked through the back doors and remembered that someone had stood out there, just the night before, and photographed me. As much as I didn't want to think about it, there was a threat against me. Even if I wasn't the intended target, I sure was stuck in the crossfire.

None of this was about me. Not the threat, not the protection. It was all about him. My father.

Through the light of the setting sun, a figure moved quickly toward doors. Heart pounding, I slid from my stool and backed away until I stood in the shadow of the entrance hall.

If this was someone looking for me, I'd run out the front door. I could make a quick escape and worry about the house... never. There was literally nothing in the house I actually cared about.

The figure moved right up to the doors until their shadow stretched across the floor, almost touching my feet, then opened the door and stepped in.

The breath left me in a rush as a sweat-soaked Logan slipped his shirt over his head and used it to mop his forehead. Muscles. Lots of muscles.

His biceps bulged as he dragged the shirt over his neck and down his ribbed stomach, and I wondered what kind of discipline he needed to maintain that kind of definition. He was a masterpiece. The kind of body you'd expect to see on the cover of one of the romance novels I had on my bookshelves upstairs. No discrete covers for me. If people didn't like what I was reading, they could fuck off.

He turned to close the door behind him, and I barely suppressed a gasp at the sight of a scar that sloped from the crease of his neck diagonally down to the back of his right hip. The edges of it looked rough, as though the medic who had tended him hadn't had much skin to work with. I shuddered, wondering what the story behind it was, and considered leaving him his privacy.

The merry beeping of the microwave took us both by surprise. Logan whipped around, immediately spotting me in the entrance hall, then moved toward the kitchen in search of the unexpected noise.

"It's the microwave. There's a plate of dinner in the fridge for you too, if you're hungry," I said, following him into the tight space in case he decided to pull a gun on the whitegoods. He grunted, pulling his shirt back on and checking my heated plate—as though worried it could still pose a threat.

"Look, I think we got off to a bad start. Go wash up, and I'll heat your plate up. We can have dinner together and get to know each other."

He eyed me cautiously, as though wondering what the motivation behind the offer was. I couldn't have told him, because I didn't know myself. All I knew was that I was spending the next however long with a guy I was insanely attracted to but knew nothing about. This was going to either be an exercise in getting along or identifying a fatal flaw I could take advantage of. I honestly couldn't have said which.

"Deal," he said finally, brushing past me and pulling clothes out of his duffel bag.

"There are clean towels in the bathroom. Second—"

"Second door on the left. I know." He hesitated at the door and glanced over his shoulder, face softening as we made eye contact. "Thanks. I'll just be a minute."

I stared at the closed door long enough to hear the whoosh of water start on the other side. I imagined seeing that chest and back, and maybe more of him covered in the fall of shower water.

"Stop it," I snapped, pulling my attention back to the kitchen and the cold plate I had promised to heat.

The hissing of the shower cut off just as the microwave called job done, and I pulled out some cutlery, setting up two spaces on the counter to eat.

The fragrant spices of the curry made my mouth water, and I turned expectantly when the click of the bathroom door signaled time to eat.

"That smells amazing," he said, sliding onto the stool beside me.

I nodded, distracted by the way his shirt clung to his chest. He'd obviously been in a hurry to eat. Water still beaded on the side of his neck, and he'd left his hat and sunglasses in the bathroom. His hair was a sandy blond, slicked back and still wet from the shower, and his eyes... a sherry red-brown color that looked far too warm on his strong face. No wonder he covered up so much. He could be mistaken for a nice guy otherwise.

"What?" he asked, his lips quirking at the corner as I continued to watch him.

"Just thinking you look nicer without your hat."

"Is that a compliment?"

I laughed. He acted like the answer didn't matter, but it hadn't escaped my notice that his fork had stopped halfway to his mouth.

"Not at all. Just that you could lull someone into a false sense of security if they didn't know better."

He grunted, biting down on his fork and speaking through his mouthful of food. "And let me guess. You know better?"

"Of course."

We ate in silence, which was surprisingly companionable, and I wondered what kind of information Logan was feeding my father. It couldn't have been much. General Walker had far more important things to worry about than his daughter. Even a stalker couldn't slow him down.

"Has there been any sign of the guy who sent the key?" I asked as casually as I could.

We had confirmed the key I found in the envelope the night before fit the front door, and Logan had replaced the lock with a biometric system that only he and I could access. Not even my father could get into the house at the moment. I had advocated for Luciana to have access, but he insisted we would control her access until the threat was "neutralized."

"Nothing so far. I'll continue to monitor things and see if we can't flush them out. Speaking of protective measures, are you ready to tell me where you went today?"

"Nope."

"You realize I need to know where you are to be able to protect you, right?"

My temper flared, and it took a considerable effort to keep any reaction from my face. I didn't need protecting. I wasn't some stupid damsel who couldn't look after herself.

But it's not about you, remember?

Taking a couple of deep breaths, I pushed chickpeas around my bowl as I considered my reply.

"When you enlisted, you were given a contract to sign. You knowingly and willingly signed away your freedom in order to fight for your country. You signed up to take orders, and in return, you became part of something bigger than yourself. The people you work with bond through shared experience and come to know you better than your family. Sometimes better than yourself." I paused, glancing over to see Logan was watching me closely with his brow furrowed. Maybe I wasn't making sense, but I needed him to understand.

"I never signed that contract. You don't get my secrets because you want them, and you certainly don't have my permission to report my life to your employer for the sake of something that has absolutely nothing to do with me."

"You're the one under threat here. You're the target—"

"No. I'm not. I'm an unwilling pawn in a bullshit game of politics. If I had anywhere else to go, I'd be there. If this little stalking matter were unlikely to reflect poorly on my father, he wouldn't care either. In his perfect world, you would be his son and I wouldn't exist, so excuse me if I'm not inclined to follow the rules of his game. Turns out, I'm not hungry."

Before he could react, I pushed away my bowl and strode toward the stairs.

So much for starting over.

4

LOGAN

*S*he had a point.

Her feet slapped against the stairs as she made her exit, and all I could do was sit and stare into my cooling bowl of curry.

She may have been a brat with daddy issues and secrets that were going to compromise her to the point of insanity—mine, not hers—but she hadn't signed up for any of it. I still wanted to spank her ass so hard she couldn't sit for a week, but maybe I needed to try something different. A softer approach than I would normally take when assignments didn't fall in line the way they should have.

After scraping up the last of my meal, and finishing off Avery's because I hated seeing food go to waste, I decided on a new plan. One that would either bring her around to my way of thinking, or at the very least let her see me as someone other than her father's spy in the house.

After washing up our bowls and cutlery, I took my laptop into the General's study and logged on to check in for my daily briefing.

The study was large and admittedly a little ostentatious for my tastes. It had the good ol' boy vibes with huge cushioned chairs beside the fireplace, a wetbar in the corner of the room, and a huge mahogany desk with a wingback chair in the center looking out over everything.

"Tanner. How's the first day gone? Any trouble?" General Walker asked as soon as his audio connected.

I thought about Avery's blow up. Her disappearance at the mall. The pain in her eyes before she retreated upstairs for the third time today.

"All quiet here, so far. Did you get the notes I sent through earlier? I took the liberty of changing out the locks as a priority because of the security breach with the key."

The General nodded. "Good, good. I'm willing to approve the surveillance equipment you suggested. Send me a quote when you have it. The text from yesterday came from a burner cell. Pinged off a tower near the house, which is no surprise. We knew the asshole was in my yard. Anything else of note?"

"I think Avery might chafe under this level of security sooner rather than later—"

"Avery will do as she's told. Just let her hide in her room, or if she's making a fuss, take her shopping." A feminine voice in the background called the General's attention away, and when he refocused, he was already moving to close our conversation.

"You're doing well, son. Keep her contained and resolve the situation as best you can. I'm going to be busy with the campaign for the next few months—and busy with something else for the next couple of hours." He winked, and I suppressed a cringe at the inference. "So keep Avery quiet and don't let her fuck things up for me. I've set up your salary and the first payment should come through on Tuesday. In the drawer to your left, there should be a Mastercard. Use that for any other incidental expenses. Same time tomorrow."

He closed the virtual meeting before I could acknowledge his instructions. There was no need for acknowledgement, though. I was a good soldier who took orders well. Just like Avery said. I signed up for this shit.

The Mastercard was right where he said it would be, but I didn't feel right taking it. I'd invoice him for the security instruments, so there was no need to use it for anything else.

Sitting in the General's study, I considered his attitude toward his daughter, hell, to women in general. It occurred to me that he had always been like that. Dismissive. Demeaning. I respected the man for everything he had achieved and everything he had given me, but I couldn't get Avery's words out of my head. Of course, he cared about his daughter. That's what parents did. Maybe he wasn't good with his words.

Ignoring the voice that muttered *bullshit* in the back of my head, I made a plan for an outing that I hoped would build trust with Avery and make my job a little easier to handle.

I HAD NEVER BEEN A GOOD SLEEPER, EVEN AS A CHILD. My parents had been at their wits' end, trying every trick in the book. I drank warm milk every night, exercised to the point of physical exhaustion every day, never watched television or played video games, and had been slathered in lavender oil so many times I couldn't stand the smell as an adult. When I joined the Army, I found my place. Sleep was irregular and unpredictable, and no one blinked an eye at a soldier being awake at midnight. While others bitched and complained about night ops and long tours, I was in my element.

After my debrief with the General, I wasted a few hours researching surveillance technology before catching three hours sleep on the sofa in the lounge. I woke refreshed and ready to start the day at around three a.m. Unable to leave for my usual nighttime run, I ran a few laps of the property instead and found a spot on the grass to work on some functional training. By the time I was finished, my limbs trembled, and my heart pounded in that delicious way that made me feel alive. I showered and made myself a snack, set the coffeepot to brew, and wondered how much longer I would let Avery sleep before I dragged her out of bed.

Seven-thirty turned out to be my limit. I ignored the sense of anticipation I felt when I climbed the stairs. I was looking forward to messing with her. It had nothing to do with wanting to see her. In that vein, I didn't care what her reaction would be to the plans for the day. I had to protect her, so she had to come with me. Simple as that.

The first knock was as polite as I was capable of and elicited no response. The second was a little harder.

The whirlwind I was expecting threw open the door, hair as wild as the day before and eyes set to burn me to a crisp. Her pouty lips parted and just as I was ready for a tongue lashing—not the fun kind—she visibly pulled herself up.

Instead, she turned her frown into a saccharine grin. "We regret to inform you that we are closed at this time. Come back when the sun is up."

I chuckled, catching the door as she tried to slam it. "The sun is up."

"I meant directly overhead. You know, the time of day normal people wake up?"

Her cheeks were flushed with color, and I couldn't help but notice she was back in the white tee and short shorts she'd been wearing the day before. *Focus.*

"The day's more than half over by then. Come on, get dressed. We have plans."

"My plans include bed," she grumbled, moving away from the door.

"Not anymore. Don't make me come in there."

"You're not my daddy."

Instant. Boner.

Fuck.

Rearranging myself with a discreet motion, I reminded myself my job was to protect the brat, not tame her. Better to disengage.

"You have ten minutes. I'll have coffee ready for you downstairs."

The muffled "you'd better" was accompanied by the rustle of clothing, so I graciously decided to let it slide as I headed downstairs to wait.

You can't have her. She may not even be into the same scene as you.

There was a point. As frustrating as these new fantasies of my assignment were, they were nothing compared to the possible disappointment of finding a vanilla playmate. Control in the bedroom was my vice, the same way alcohol was for Damon.

Shit. I wondered how he was going. I'd checked in with Bear a couple of days ago, but no one had heard from Damon since the morning after Adrien's funeral. Talk about a shit friend. I made a mental note to call him to organize a catch-up after all this stalker business was put to bed.

My morose thoughts screeched to a halt with the appearance of Avery in a tank top and Daisy Dukes. Her pale hair was pulled into a messy knot on top of her head, tendrils escaping to brush against her throat as she reached for the coffee mug I offered in tribute.

"Come on, time to go," I urged after she'd taken a long drink. "We can get breakfast on the way."

She rolled her eyes, huffing through her nose, but followed me out to my truck with her coffee mug cradled in her hand.

"Where are we going, anyway?" she asked, buckling her belt and glancing across the space between us. Her eyes were wary, and I wondered how she was going to react to the plans.

"You'll see." I started the truck, ignoring the way her eyes narrowed at me as we peeled out of the driveway.

Ten minutes from our destination, I pulled into a small diner that was known for their breakfast bagels and treated Avery to a bite to eat and another coffee.

"How do you not jitter when you walk?" I asked, eyeing the jumbo cup she had ordered to take away as we headed back to my truck.

"Quite easily. I'm usually asleep at this time, so you're interacting with the caffeine, not Avery. Enjoy. Caffeine can be a bitch."

I snorted, pulling the door open for her before circling the truck and climbing in on my side.

"Good to know."

Seven minutes later, we pulled onto the dirt road that led to my run-down farmhouse. *This is a good idea*, I promised myself, glancing at Avery as I flicked on my turn signal.

Her face showed a whole lot of nothing, but I hoped I could change that.

"You were right," I said as we rolled to a stop in front of the dilapidated building.

"I usually am, but what time are you referring to?"

I huffed a laugh, trying to keep the smile from my face. "I'm asking for a lot of faith from you when we know very little about each other, so I thought we could start here."

I gestured to the sagging porch.

"At a run-down farm that looks like it'll blow over in the next storm?"

This was a stupid idea. Of course, she wouldn't understand that I didn't let anyone into my personal space. I knew I would have to get over the hang-up when it came to rewiring and plumbing the place, but I hadn't shown anyone this little project or shared my long-term plans. Until now.

"Sorry," she said, putting a hand on my arm.

"I voluntarily discharged from the Army last week."

Why was that so hard to say? I didn't regret the decision. I knew I was done with that part of my life, but the sense I was adrift without the structure of my old life had been unexpected. Renovating this old farm was my new purpose. It was something that kept me sane when the nights felt too long.

"Ok."

"This place is... my anchor."

"Ok." The understanding in the word the second time she said it was hard to hear. I pushed out of the truck, avoiding her eyes, and circled around to open her door and give her a hand down.

"Today's demo day. Hope you're ready to get dirty, hen."

Her grin was unexpected. The enthusiasm with which she jumped out of my truck, even more so.

"Always keen to get all messed up. Especially if it means I get to break things."

She was as good as her word. Armed with a mallet each, we demolished the kitchen and main bathroom, hauling cabinets and fixtures to the dumpster I had hired for the occasion. At around one o'clock, I stopped us for a lunch break. I expected her to run for the truck, ready to get away from the heat and the mess of the job. Instead, she volunteered to clean up while I ran into town.

I returned thirty minutes later with burgers and soda to find her singing while she swept. Her voice was deep and seductive as she moved the broom across the floor, her hips swiveling in time to the lyrics. She was completely relaxed, seemingly enjoying the hard work, and I struggled to reconcile her with the girl I'd heard about for years. Finishing the song, she turned, then shrieked when she caught sight of me looming in the doorway.

I held my hands up, trying to placate her. "Just me. Sorry. I brought food." I waved the burger bag like a white flag.

She pressed her hand to her chest and slumped over the broom. "What the hell were you doing? You scared the hell out of me."

I felt my cheek tug into a reluctant smile. "You are nothing like I expected you to be, Avery Walker."

"Thank you?" She tilted her head, as though she weren't entirely sure what to make of me, before stepping past me on her way out the front door. "Where are you going?"

"To wash up. And so should you. We're both filthy."

My breath caught as my mind flew to other scenarios that would make us filthy dirty. Clearing my throat, I followed after her, subtly brushing my hand across the front of my pants to make sure the effect she was having on me wasn't visible.

"So... Stevie Nicks, huh?" I asked as we settled on the grass next to the front stoop.

One day, I would have a deck wrapped all the way around the farmhouse, but today all I had was some rotting wooden planks that threatened splinters at best for anyone brave enough to take a seat.

From the back windows of the house, the land fell away into a valley. Lush green hills rolled out as far as the eye could see, making you feel like you stood at the edge of the world. The view was part of the appeal of the property. The isolation was a close second. I wondered if Avery appreciated it, or if she was already chafing to get back to her immaculate place of residence.

"I love her music," Avery said, taking a bite of her cheeseburger and glancing around the yard.

"I thought you'd be into One Direction or Bieber or something."

"Ew, gag. I have taste in music, thank you very much. Stevie's songs have meaning. They have heart. You can feel the energy in the lyrics when you sing them. Words have power, you know?"

I nodded, pretending I had any idea what she was talking about.

"What do you listen to?" she asked, turning the conversation back to me.

"Whatever's on the radio," I said with a shrug. She snorted, taking another bite of her lunch.

"What?"

The look she gave me was equal parts pity and something else I didn't quite understand.

"You're just like my dad, is all. God, no wonder he loves you."

She had told me before that her dad preferred me, and I wished I could have refuted the claim, but I was beginning to realize General Walker didn't know his daughter very well. A squirrel skittered down a nearby tree and high-tailed it across the yard as quickly as its furry butt could move as I tried to grasp what Avery had meant by her comment. I felt like I had failed some kind of test.

She watched me quietly as my pride battled with my need to know more. Taking pity on me, she sighed, screwing up her empty burger wrapper.

"Art is all about creation. Painting, dance... music. From a single spark of inspiration, some people can create whole worlds, stories so richly communicated through different mediums that it deliberately draws the emotions of witnesses to that art. Everything in nature has a story. It makes the world a more interesting place to live in and encourages us to be curious. There are a lot of creators in the world. There are also people like my dad."

The answer hit me like a blow to the head, and the idea she saw me that way caused the burger I'd just eaten to turn to lead in my gut.

"Destroyers."

She nodded. "Some people don't appreciate creation. Sometimes they actively set out to unmake what someone so painstakingly brought to life. It's not their fault, the world is about balance, but..."

I nodded, thinking about the teddy bear on the grave. Adrien and Damon. Shit. Every tour of duty I'd been on in the last decade. She was right. I destroyed everything I touched. I glanced at the farmhouse behind me. Wasn't I trying to change that, though? After demolition came renovation. Breaking something down to its workable parts to build it up better than before. I had to believe there was a possibility for growth, for learning, or I may as well have followed Adrien's lead.

"I shouldn't have said anything. I'm sorry," Avery said, standing and brushing dirt from her ass.

I followed her more slowly, my mind still churning over the idea of creation and destruction.

"Hey," she said, laying a tentative hand on my arm. Her fingers were cool against my heated skin, and I ignored how nice they felt in favor of focusing on her face.

"Let's get some more work done here, then there's something I want to show you back at the house, okay?"

I didn't like the shift that had occurred in our dynamic. I was the one who was always in control. Instead of acknowledging the cracks she had chipped on my armor, I grunted, shrugging off her hand and heading back toward the house. Vaulting onto the porch, I pushed my way into the house without looking over my shoulder, even though every fiber of my being hoped she was following.

What the fuck was I getting myself into?

5

AVERY

*W*e passed the afternoon in silence, each of us choosing a different room to work in. I cursed myself again for mentioning my theory of creation and destruction. No matter how true it was, someone who had a conscience never wanted to hear they were going to break anything they touched. At least, in that way, he was different from my dad. That man reveled in destroying things, especially when it happened in the shadows, leaving his reputation squeaky clean.

Now that I'd met Logan and gotten to know him some, I hoped he wasn't a toy my father wanted to corrupt. He may have been growly and standoffish, with a hint of something under the surface that made my blood run hot, but I didn't think he was a bad person.

When the setting sunlight stretched across what was left of the tiles I was removing from the bathroom floor, I powered down the jackhammer I'd been using and stretched my aching back. My shoulders hummed with fatigue as I swung my arms to loosen my tight muscles, stretching my neck from one side to the other.

"How are you feeling?"

The shriek that left my mouth—for the second time in one freaking day—was feral and not at all tough or womanly. Logan leaned against the doorframe, smirking in that infuriatingly attractive way of his.

"Stop doing that!" I yelled, slapping his chest hard enough to hurt my hand.

Damn it, I knew better than to hit like that. Subtly rubbing the sting out of my skin, I shouldered past him, desperate to place some space between us.

He caught my hand as I stepped through the door, turning it to inspect the newly formed calluses at the base of each finger.

"You did well today. I really appreciate your help. I couldn't have gotten anywhere near as much done by myself," he said, massaging my palm with strong fingers.

He kept his eyes on what he was doing as I tried to remember how to breathe. No one had ever given me a hand massage before, and it felt as though each stroke was sending electric shocks straight to my pussy.

Down, girl.

He adjusted his grip and continued to work, flicking his eyes up and back as the silence stretched. I swallowed, trying to work some spit into my suddenly dry mouth.

"I was happy to." Why did that sound like an offer? I hoped he couldn't hear the arousal in my voice.

Self-preservation urged me to break the contact, but perhaps I was a masochist because I offered him my other hand with zero resistance when he finished with the first. We stood so close; my breath ruffled his sweat damp hair. I wondered where he had ditched his hat. Then I didn't care about anything as he hit a particularly tight muscle, and I didn't swallow my moan fast enough. We both froze.

"Thanks," I breathed, breaking the moment.

Pulling my hand out of his, I stood back, wiping it self-consciously on the ass of my shorts as though it could wipe away my reaction to him.

He cleared his throat, rubbing his own hands on his thighs and looking around the room like he needed an escape.

"Hungry?" he offered.

"Starving," I whispered before catching myself. Shit.

The growl that rumbled out of his throat sent shivers down my spine, even as I was possessed with the need to run. Fast.

"Umm... Luciana left us plenty of meals to heat up at home."

He nodded, accepting the change of topic, and steered me out of the house with a hand on my lower back.

The car ride passed in a charged silence. My skin tingled, hyperaware of the man beside me. The way he gripped the steering wheel, how his shoulders seemed to fill so much of the cab. When I worked up the courage to send the quickest of glances at his crotch, I wondered if the peak in his pants weren't an erection just begging for my mouth.

"You need to stop looking at me like that, hen. You won't like the consequences."

I hummed noncommittally, begging to differ. I was quite sure I'd be very happy with any consequences he wanted to give me.

When we arrived at home, I was too worked up to eat, but Logan refused to hear otherwise. I sat, picking at my plate under his watchful eye until he decided I'd waited long enough.

"What was it you wanted to show me?" he asked, clearing our plates from the table and placing them carefully in the sink.

A wicked fantasy flashed in my mind. Me on my knees for him, worshipping his cock while he praised me. Maybe choked me, just a little.

It took an enormous amount of will to let the vision go. That wasn't who we were to each other. It didn't mean I couldn't pretend later in the night when I was alone in my room.

Not trusting my voice, I beckoned for him to follow me upstairs and began to climb.

My favorite space in the entire house was the attic. A room I had converted, by myself, into an oasis.

"This is..." Logan's voice trailed off as his eyes swept around the space. I wondered how he saw it.

Across the space, a floor-to-ceiling window looked out over the back lawn. Positioned to make the best use of the light were my easel and paint supplies. A huge worktable stretched a third of the way across the left wall and was cluttered with everything from my mini pottery wheel and ceramic tools to pencils, charcoal, and old paint pallets. A kiln sat on the right-hand side of the window, currently unlit, but in winter it worked better than a heater to keep the space warm.

Closer to the door was a stretch of open floor covered in padding that made you feel like you were walking on springs. I'd never needed it, really, though when I laid it, I'd had a vague idea of using the area for sparring one day. To my right was my prized possession. To the uneducated, it could have been mistaken for a hat rack, but it had nothing to do with clothing.

I fidgeted, feeling oddly exposed as I showed Logan who I truly was. Not the façade everyone else got to see. God, I was going to puke.

"You know what? How about we just forget this and go downstairs," I said, pushing at him to go back downstairs. I was about as successful as I would have been trying to lift his truck.

He moved into the room, ignoring my huff of frustration, and gravitated toward my worktable.

"I expected a lot more clothes, or... something..." he said, poking his finger into the cloth-covered block of clay I left out the night before after making a fruit bowl. I slapped his hand away, and he moved farther down toward some half-completed watercolor paintings.

"These are good."

I flushed at the compliment, unsure how to take it. When I was younger, before Mom left, Dad thought my art was a passing fancy. He probably thought, much like Logan, that I'd converted the attic into a giant wardrobe for the clothing he assumed I bought in excess. I might have encouraged the belief, but it was mostly because it was the easiest way to get him to leave me alone.

Logan crossed his arms over his chest and leaned his ass against the table, watching me too closely for comfort. Beneath the bill of his hat, his eyes looked almost black, and I wondered what the hell I'd been thinking bringing him up here.

He shifted, and I couldn't help but notice the way his arms bulged with the movement. I swallowed hard, my anxiety over showing this private space to him, combined with my very real attraction for him, overwhelming me to the point of near panic.

"Do I scare you, hen?" he asked.

"No."

The edge of his mouth quirked, and he crooked a finger at me. The pull was irresistible. With my heart pounding in my chest, I crossed the room until we were standing toe to toe. He dropped his hands to the table behind him and shifted so that his knees framed my hips. My foot twitched with the need to move, but I wasn't certain whether I wanted to be closer or if I wanted to run.

His eyes dropped to my mouth as I licked my lips.

"Are you sure?"

I was positive I wasn't just scared. I was terrified, and so wet it was a wonder there was any moisture left in my body.

"Kneel."

I dropped so fast I knew there would be bruises on my knees come morning. I didn't care. The move put me eye level with his crotch, and this time, there was no doubt that he and I were on the same page. His zipper strained against the bulge beneath it.

Squeezing my thighs together to lessen the ache in my core, I watched his face through my lashes, looking for clues about where he wanted this to go.

"Have you played like this before, hen?" he asked.

I shook my head. I hadn't experienced it personally, but I had read about it, fantasized about it. Watched it in a dozen porn scenes. My hands shook with anticipation as he maintained his position.

Touch me. Use me. Do something! I screamed at him in my mind, but I knew enough about the game to keep quiet.

With all the leisure of someone out for an afternoon stroll, Logan straightened from his lean and dropped into a crouch so that we were nose to nose.

"We'll have to go slow, then. Take off your shirt for me. Let me see you."

In a flourish of movement that was almost ruined when my shirt caught on the underside of my breasts, I shed my t-shirt, dropping it on the floor beside me. Logan's eyes didn't leave mine.

Was this a test?

"Beautiful," he growled.

With a feather-soft touch, he traced his hand up my arm, fingers dancing along my collarbone, up my throat, and across my cheek. In a move that stole the breath from my body, his hand tightened in my hair, and his mouth crashed down on mine. The kiss was punishing. More fight than affection, as though he were angry with the turn circumstances had taken.

I wanted to give it right back, but found myself softening under his bruising lips, absorbing the ferocity of teeth and tongue until all I could do was keep a grip on the front of his shirt and hold on. It took long moments for me to realize the mewling sounds that dusted the air around us were coming from my own throat. I wanted this. I wanted him.

Reaching behind me, I loosened the clasp on my bra, freeing my breasts in the hopes of moving things along.

I was ready.

And then he was gone.

Between one breath and the next he was on his feet, striding toward the door. On the threshold, he turned, eyes trained above where I kneeled topless and vulnerable in the middle of the floor.

"That shouldn't have happened. You're my assignment, and the only way I can effectively do my job is if I keep emotions out of it. This wasn't your fault."

I gaped at the empty space he had just occupied, wondering what the hell had just happened.

My body throbbed, furious at being denied what seemed like a certainty such a short time ago. Well, fuck him very much. I could get myself off.

Crawling under my worktable, I pulled out one of many shoeboxes I had stashed under there as storage. This one had something a little more intimate in it.

With a last look at the empty doorway, I loosened the button on my shorts and braced forearm on the edge of the table, pulling my magic bullet out of its box with the other hand. Its buzzing filled the air, and I almost whimpered with relief as I shoved the device inside my underwear, already embarrassingly slick from my encounter with Logan.

The familiar pulses sent shivers up my spine, and I moaned as my hips fell into an unconscious rhythm. I imagined Logan walking back into the room. Imagined those reddish eyes watching me take control of my own pleasure, not asking his permission or seeking approval. My stomach lurched as the sensations ratcheted up a notch as I stared down fantasy Logan, defying him and challenging him to stop me.

In my mind, he growled, just like he had in real life. He told me to stop. To be a good girl and wait for my pleasure. I flipped him off and moved the toy to my entrance, teasing the sensitive flesh as my nerve endings fired to the point of pain. I bit my lip, imagining Logan surrendering with a rabid look on his face. His hands ripping at the fly of his pants and pulling out the length I could only guess at. As he shoved his cock down my throat, I came with an unapologetic scream.

I didn't care if real-life Logan could hear me downstairs. In fact... I wanted him to.

He thought I was a brat before?

I'd show him how bratty I could be.

Logan Tanner had chosen to hide from what we both so clearly wanted. He was acting like a coward, so I was back to plan A. Make his life hell.

I wondered how long he'd last before he cracked.

I couldn't wait to see.

6

LOGAN

*D*espite my best intentions, I found myself backtracking to the top of the stairs after I stormed out of the room. Fine, I'd hightailed it out of there like a bitch. My head was a mess, and I struggled to think objectively about what had happened. I was attracted to her. Of course, I was. She was fucking gorgeous, but it was more than that. She was funny. Smart. Full of surprises.

I had never questioned General Walker. Ever. About anything. And now I was confronted with the irrefutable proof that he was wrong about his own daughter. She wasn't vapid or flighty. She seemed to not give a shit about clothes or things. I didn't know what she was doing during all those shopping trips he talked about, but unless all of them were to art supply stores, she sure as hell wasn't shopping.

The way she had obeyed my orders was probably the biggest head fuck of all. Here was a girl who was supposed to be pure. The virgin type. I knew how the General trotted her out as the lady of the house at his shindigs. But the way she had dropped to her knees, eyeing my cock like it was a fucking ice cream on a hot day? She submitted perfectly for someone who had never played with power dynamics in the bedroom. The image of those hazel eyes staring up at me through her lashes was going to haunt me for the foreseeable future.

A low buzzing started up in the room behind me, and I wondered which art medium she'd decided to work in.

Then I heard her breath catch and release on a long sigh.

My head snapped around so fast my neck screamed in protest, the rest of my body frozen as my mind went to war.

Don't go in there. Just walk away. Now.

Fuck you. How can I not?

And so, I stayed put, torn between staying and leaving. Hanging on every groan and whimper until a scream echoed down the stairwell. Not wanting to be caught like the peeping tom I fucking was, I ghosted downstairs as quickly and silently as I could. I gathered a change of clothing and put myself in an ice-cold shower.

The great thing about cold showers: the shock of that icy flow on overheated skin wiped your brain clean while you tried to remember how to breathe.

The bad thing? All those thoughts came flooding back the second you wrapped a towel around you when you hopped out. Rather than pulling on the fresh shorts and t-shirt I had brought into the bathroom with me, I wandered out to my bag and found a pair of basketball shorts instead. If I couldn't wash away the image of Avery on her knees... the sound she made when she made herself come... I'd exercise until I physically couldn't climb the stairs and order her back into her rightful position at my feet.

&.

"LOGAN, PLEASE." THE VOICE REACHED THROUGH MY chest, wrapping around my heart like a fist, ready to squeeze as everything flashed white.

I came awake on a gasp, flinging a hand out to catch myself before I rolled off the sofa. Shit.

My ears rang with remembered pain, and my heart pounded, as though making up for the beats missed in the dream. Hauling myself into a seated position, I sucked deep breaths in through my nose, reminding myself that there was no immediate danger. I wasn't back on deployment. Memories could not hurt me. Much.

I didn't have to glance at the time, but did out of habit, glaring at the 2:22 as though the numbers themselves were responsible for my continued insomnia. The only nights I didn't wake at 2:22 were the ones I didn't sleep at all. The Army psych they had wanted me to see would've had a field day with my sleep patterns.

I'd seen the middle-aged white male, who had clearly spent the decades between gaining his degree and finding me in his office sitting behind a desk and not in the field of combat. In the initial assessment meeting—the only one I'd attended due to the threat of disciplinary action if I didn't—he'd thrown around acronyms like confetti. CPTSD and OCD got a fair run before he'd launched into the bright idea to schedule shit and change my "thinking patterns." Once he'd really warmed up, he'd hit me with the medication one/two punch, and with that, I was out the door with an apology about conflicting appointments.

What the fuck had that guy known, anyway?

As my heart rate slowed to around normal pace, I wandered out through the French doors on to the patio. I frowned, glancing up at the attic window. Light streamed through the glass, and I wondered if maybe Avery had left the light on when she went to bed. A shadow moved past the window, stretching long over the lawn, and I realized I wasn't the only sleepless one in the house.

A moment later, the light extinguished, plunging the yard into darkness.

"Bedtime, I guess," I muttered, scratching my chest and backtracking into the house to retrieve a flashlight.

I'd walk the property, check the cameras, and then do some yoga or something. I always managed to find a way to fill the night hours, and no doubt, the General would want an update sooner rather than later.

The grass was cool and slightly damp under my bare feet as I padded toward the nearest wall and ambled along the property line. A dog barked in the distance; its call echoed by another canine voice farther off. Who knew the suburbs were so quiet in the morning hours? At the farmhouse, there was always a cacophony of frogs, hunting owls, and crickets filling the night with life and comfort. The silence reminded me too much of those long nights on deployment, when the peace of night was so often a cover for those who wanted to keep us from finding our way home. My dream flashed in my mind, but with a stubborn shake of my head, I pushed it back.

The day I'd arrived, I'd placed cameras around the property at 150-yard intervals. The steady red lights that indicated the units were working had interrupted the darkness for the first half of my walk, but between one tree and the next, the light vanished. Lifting my flashlight, I inspected the now empty branch I'd left the camera on.

Nothing.

I checked the ground around the base of the tree to see if something had displaced it, but again, found no sign of the missing technology. The same was true at the next point. When I found a broken bracket at the base of the third tree in a row, my instincts were screaming that something was amiss. Without finishing the patrol, I sprinted across the lawn back to the house and took the stairs two at a time to Avery's room. First rule of protection detail: secure the asset in the first instance.

I found her curled up under her blankets, one foot thrust out as though testing the temperature of the room. Her blonde hair spilled across her pillow, more luminous than the moonlight streaming through her pillow. A white streak of what looked like clay painted her temple, and I imagined her brushing her hair back absently while working on one of the pots I'd seen up in her art room.

She looked so innocent in sleep. So vulnerable. She made me want to protect her and force her to submit to my every dirty fantasy, all at once.

Closing her bedroom door carefully, I headed back downstairs, checked all of the locks on the doors and windows to outside, then brought up the footage from the missing cameras.

I was on my fourth cup of coffee and ready to tear my hair out by the time the sun was peeking over the horizon. I'd identified the moment when each of the cameras had been taken out—ten cameras in total—and had been unable to find footage of what had caused the interference. Each camera appeared to have gone offline at twenty-second intervals. The last coincided with the footage of me emerging from the house.

I checked the footage of cameras facing the street, but there wasn't much to see. An old silver Volvo that had been parked on the curb two doors down since the day before, a red Honda motorcycle, and a couple of garbage bins that hadn't been brought inside after collection day. No sign of anyone skulking around, no signs of life at all.

With a curse, I pulled out my cell and hit call on a number I knew I could trust.

"Hey, man, still having trouble sleeping, huh?"

"What are you talking about? Sun's up. This is a goddamned civil hour to be calling."

Bear's grunt told me he didn't buy my bullshit. Of course, he didn't. Bear didn't get his nickname because he was seven feet of solid muscle in human form. I mean… he was, but he was also the mama bear of the unit. He'd even managed to make Santa-shaped shortbreads one year when we'd been stuck in the middle of the desert. He'd had to tell us what the deformed things were supposed to be, and the finished product tasted like dirt, but the fact remained that he was a dude completely attuned to his unit and eager to help.

The annoying-as-shit thing? He was also patient as hell.

After an extended silence, I gave up the posturing.

"Fine. So... you know I took that job babysitting the General's daughter? Turns out, there may be an actual threat. Overnight, someone has managed to disable half of the surveillance I set up around the house. I've been over all the footage and there's no evidence. Not a single frame of imagery of whoever did it. I was hoping you could help with... Fuck, I don't even know."

"You didn't think there was a real threat?"

"I thought this assignment was a knee-jerk reaction. We've heard stories for years about how bratty Avery is. I thought she might have set up the stalker line as a bid for attention. She clearly has daddy issues—"

I ran a hand through my hair. Shit, where was my cap? Turning to look for my missing headgear, I locked eyes with the woman in question, frozen at the bottom of the staircase.

"Shit." Before I could say anything, she was across the room, headed for the front door. There was a jingle of keys, a slam, and she was gone.

"You just fucked up. Didn't you?" There was no accusation in the tone. A little amusement, because he was still a dick, even if he was a dick who cared, but he wasn't judging me.

"Go after her. Also, it's not me you should be talking to. Call Damon. He'll be happy to have something to do, and you know it. Suicide isn't contagious. You can't catch it because you spoke to the family member of someone who completed it."

I cursed and hung up on him, knowing he was right but unable to think of much past the fading purr of Avery's car engine as she took off to fuck knew where.

Throwing open the front door, I stood impotently on the stoop, watching the red motorcycle tear down the road. A green minivan was parked in the spot the Volvo had occupied previously and aside from a cat snoozing on the wall a few houses down, the street looked exactly as it had on the video I'd been watching all morning.

I dialed Avery's cell number and heard the ringing in my ear echo upstairs.

The second she got home, I was confiscating her keys.

Part of me wanted to drive circles around the suburbs searching for her. Another part wanted to stand guard over the house. What if someone caught up to her when I wasn't there? What if she came home and was vulnerable to attack because I was out searching for her? Where would she go?

The answer hit me, and I was racing for my truck like my life depended on it.

Thirty minutes later, I pulled up a long, empty drive and threw my truck in park. Shit. She'd been so comfortable here the day before. The empty house seemed to laugh at my stupidity. This was my place, not hers. Of course, she wouldn't have run to the farmhouse if she were upset.

"Shit. The mall."

Throwing my truck in reverse, I pulled a messy K-turn and headed back into town. There was something in the vicinity of the mall that had meant enough to her to keep secret. Something so important, she'd already evaded my protection detail once to attend it. Breaking several speed limits, I hightailed it to the mall and breathed a sigh of relief when I spotted her yellow Volkswagen beetle snuggled between two SUVs. Parking in the next available space, I locked up my truck, stalked to her car, sat my ass on her bumper, and pulled out my cell.

"Damon."

7

AVERY

She clearly has daddy issues. I blocked and struck hard at my Chi Sao partner, over-extending my arm and allowing a strike through my guard.

"Don't fight force with force, Avery. Know when to yield and use their momentum against them," Master William chided.

I nodded, taking a conscious breath and refocusing on my sparring partner. I was better than this, but Logan was so far in my head I couldn't get into the session.

"Do you need a break?" Ben, my Chi Sao partner, asked kindly.

I wanted to say no and push through, but Master William was right. Taking a moment to clear my head was a way better strategy than letting Ben kick my inattentive ass all over the Kwoon. Grabbing my water bottle, I took a swig, leaning back against the wall to watch the others in the class paired off and engaging in their own sparring sessions.

I'd discovered Wing Chun Kung Fu a decade ago, after my mom left and I realized I was stuck in a house with a narcissist who regularly brought strange men home to show off his perfect life and perfect daughter. At the time, I'd needed to know that I could defend myself if I needed to. Nowadays, it was my escape from all my stressors.

Master William had asked me to start working in the children's class as a Si-hing, or student-teacher, the year before. I loved the teaching and the learning. Today, it wasn't going to be enough, though.

Not only had Logan left me half naked and completely worked up the night before, but to hear he thought I was a brat with daddy issues really rubbed me the wrong way. He wasn't that much older than me, and I knew for a fact this attraction wasn't one sided. What the hell was his problem, anyway?

I was still fuming ten minutes later when Master William called the class to a close.

"Is there anything you wish to speak about?" he asked as students filed out of the Kwoon, each taking a moment to bow on the threshold before wandering out into the midday sun.

"No. I'm just preoccupied with home stuff. I'm sorry I brought it in here."

Master William smiled. "Meditate on it. Reconnect your mind and body and come back tomorrow centered and ready to train." I nodded, opening my mouth to respond, but he held his hand up. "If you're still unable to focus, beat the hell out of your dummy... the wooden one, or the one who has you distracted. Either way."

I choked on a laugh as he turned away, a twinkle in his eye.

"Tomorrow, Si-hing Avery."

"Tomorrow, Si-gong. Have a good night." I bowed as I stepped through the doorway and wandered back toward the mall parking lot.

"Avery."

I turned at the sound of my name, frowning as a dark-haired man jogged after me. I adjusted my stance, ready to defend myself if needed.

He slowed as he reached me, doubling over to breathe as though he'd chased me a ways before he caught me. "Avery, hey. I thought it was you. How are you doing?"

I frowned, edging back a step.

"Who are you?"

"Oh, sorry. Hi. I'm Damon. I used to work with your dad. I should have started with that. Weird guy chasing you down in the parking lot? Duh." He slapped his forehead and gave a self-deprecating smile.

"So, were you shopping just now?" he asked, straightening and taking a step back in a way that made me wonder if he was trying to appear non-threatening. Or maybe I was paranoid, and this was literally just someone saying *hi, I know your parents*.

"I... Yeah, just doing some window shopping. Dad's birthday is coming up and all..."

"Oh, yeah." He closed the distance between us, cupping my elbow and waving me on. "It's in a couple of weeks, right? Hey, can I walk you to your car?"

Suddenly, wires connected in my mind. Damon. He was the one who... "Hey, I'm sorry about your brother."

He froze, his hand on my elbow squeezing to the point of pain. Shrugging out of his grasp, I turned, stepping backward to reestablish the gap between us.

"Yeah. Me too," he murmured.

"Hey—" Whatever he was going to say was interrupted by the ringing of his cell.

"Logan. Hi," he said, connecting the call.

I'm not here, I mouthed stupidly at him. How could Logan possibly know I had randomly run into Damon while out and about?

He frowned at me but gave me a nod as he tuned into the conversation. "Sure, I'll take a look. Yeah. Yeah, just send over what you've got. I'll work my magic and see what comes up. Sure. See you soon."

It occurred to me that I had no reason to stand there and wait for him to finish his call. Taking advantage of his distraction, I waved and strode off toward my car.

Turning into the aisle that held my car, I noticed a hulking body relaxing over my beautiful yellow paint job.

"I swear to God, if you chipped my paint..." The rest of my sentence was muffled by t-shirt as I was pulled into a fierce, unexpected hug.

"What the fuck were you thinking, hen?" he asked, pulling back and looking me over.

"I was thinking you're an asshole, and I needed some space."

"You don't get space while there's a threat out there against you. Pull that kind of shit again and I'll put you over my knee and spank you."

I ignored the flare of heat that shivered through me. I was angry at this guy. How dare he order me around after what he'd said and done over the last twenty-four hours?

"You think that'll tame this brat?" I spat the word at him, wanting him to know that he'd hurt me. "Joke's on you. I'm into that shit."

No, damn it. I wasn't supposed to say that last part.

Instead of revoking what had been aired, I flounced to the driver's side door and slipped into my car. Logan caught my door before I could close it, leaning in over me until he was all I could see. Shit, he smelled good.

"Go straight home," he growled. "I'll be right behind you." He slammed my door and stormed away, taking all the oxygen in my car with him.

With a shaking hand, I turned on the ignition and drove home, feeling like wolves were biting at my heels. As soon as I stepped out of my car in the front drive, Logan was there, hand extended.

"You can't be trusted with your keys. I'm keeping them from now on."

"Fuck you."

He sighed, squeezing the bridge of his nose as though his head hurt.

"Avery, please. Just cooperate for once in your life. I'm trying to keep you safe."

"It seems a lot more like you're trying to control me. You know, keep me in line so I'm not an embarrassment to my father? God, is it dark with your head shoved that far up his ass?" I shouldered past him and stormed into the house.

The day was warm, and as soon as I began peeling my workout clothes from my body, I realized exactly how I wanted to spend the afternoon. If it happened to be a painful experience for Mr. Bossy-as-Fuck, all the better.

Wrapping my robe around my shoulders, I wandered downstairs and around the side of the house to the pool area. It may have been invisible from the back doors, but I knew exactly where he'd put his cameras, so he was about to get a show. Loosening the tie around my waist, I stepped up to the pool's edge and let the fabric slip from my shoulders, staring into the lens of the nearest camera as I stepped naked into the water.

I ducked under the surface, reveling in the way the currents brushed against my bare skin. I'd always wanted to swim naked but had never felt safe enough to try. I hated that I felt safe with Logan, despite what he'd said, but I was going to show him exactly how bratty I could be if he kept up his pompous shit.

Up and back, up and back, I swam leisurely laps until the call of the sun was too strong. Without bothering to retrieve my robe, I lay facedown on the nearest lounger, absorbing the sun's rays as I practiced a meditation that felt easier now that I'd tired my body out.

"What do you think you're doing?"

I hadn't expected him to have the balls to show his face so soon.

"Warming my cold, bratty blood," I murmured without bothering to crack an eyelid.

The slap of his feet retreated, and I almost breathed a sigh of relief, but then they returned, and my lounger tipped as he added his weight to the edge of it.

"You'll burn if you don't put sunblock on."

A cold streak hit my back, and then large hands followed, rubbing the silky substance into my naked skin. His strong fingers worked over my shoulders and down my arms in circles before sweeping over my ribcage, barely tickling the sides of my breasts where they pressed into the cushion beneath me.

The sound of more sunblock squirting into his hand was followed by a swipe over my lower back and a slight hesitation before his touch traveled over the globes of my ass and down each leg. His fingertips brushed dangerously close to my core, and I prayed he couldn't see how much he was affecting my body. No matter what conscious decisions I had made about this man, it was glaringly obvious my body wanted what he was offering. Or not offering, as the case may be. When he'd covered every inch of the back of me, I rolled, exposing my front to him in a way I swore to myself wasn't an invitation.

My nipples peaked from the brush of a cool breeze, so at odds with the heated cognac stare of the man looming over me.

"You're playing a dangerous game here, hen," he rumbled, sweeping his gaze over my body, drinking me in as though savoring me like a fine wine.

I shrugged, stretching my hands overhead and arching my spine. No worries here, I was just enjoying the day, naked as a blue jay. Or was it jaybird?

With a smirk, he squeezed more sunblock into his hands and carefully rubbed it over my face before moving down over my neck and clavicles. His eyes caught and held mine as he slicked his hands over my breasts, circling around the mounds before taking each nipple between thumb and forefinger and twisting viciously.

I gasped, pushing up into the sensation as moisture gushed out of me, leaving a damp patch on the lounger cushion. Christ, the bite of pleasure and pain together was almost enough to make me come without any other stimulation.

He grunted, leaving me unsure if I'd passed some kind of test or failed miserably. Continuing his mission to make me sun-safe, he rubbed the cream into my stomach and over my hips. When he started on my thighs, I saw the moment he spotted the wet cushion. His eyes shot to mine, a deep frown pulling at his brow.

"No more games, little girl," he growled, hurriedly finishing each of my legs before straightening and taking a deliberate step back.

"I promise, you wouldn't be able to handle me." He turned, heading toward the house, but I refused to let him have the last word this time.

"I think you're scared *you* can't handle *me*. Don't make me responsible for your failings, Captain Tanner."

He didn't stop, or acknowledge me in any way, just strode into the house, slamming the door behind him. I sunk back into the lounger, scowling. Any good vibes I'd had were a memory, and as I looked around the yard, I shivered, feeling exposed. Retrieving my robe, I headed back toward the house at a much slower pace, ready to wash the last few minutes from my skin.

8

LOGAN

"The red motorcycle. How often has that been in the neighborhood?" Damon asked, the clacking of his keyboard drilling into my ear as his crazy smart brain worked to solve the mystery I'd found myself working through.

"I don't know. It took off around the same time as Avery this morning, but that could be a coincidence."

Damon made a rude noise. "You believe in coincidences now, do you? Shit, it's lucky you got out, or you'd get us all killed."

Smartass. It was good to hear Damon felt up to hanging shit on me. It gave me hope that we didn't bury him when we lost Adrien, but that didn't mean I was going to take it.

"Hilarious. I just don't think we should be jumping to conclusions here."

Damon hummed, the dubious noise as cutting as any reprimand. "I'm going to run the plates and do a background check on the guy, so you don't wake up dead. What other security measures are you adding? Do you need me to set something up for you?"

An image of Avery naked out by the pool flashed through my mind. Fuck. There was no way in hell I'd risk letting Damon see her like that.

My palms burned with the memory of her smooth skin. She knew exactly what she was doing. The brat was trying to push me into losing control, and I'd be damned if it wasn't working. The way she'd writhed under my hands... seeing her arousal on the cushion had been the last straw. If I'd stuck around, I would have spanked her until she couldn't sit down or fucked her raw. Probably both. I couldn't afford the distraction she provided.

"Logan?"

"Nah, man. I got it. Hit me up if you get anything on the bike, okay?"

"Will do, bud. Keep safe, yeah? Don't want to see you end up pussy whipped."

"Fuck you, Smith."

"Fuck you too, Tanner. For real, though. Keep safe. We've lost enough good people."

I shifted, uncomfortable with the direction the conversation had gone in. If anyone should be giving the stay safe message, it should be me.

Damon ended the call a minute later, citing the need to puke at all the feels I was giving him. Asshole. I grinned, stretching my arms overhead and reveling in the burn of my muscles from my workout earlier in the day.

Wandering into the kitchen, I wondered what Avery was up to. After the incident by the pool the day before, she'd disappeared upstairs, declining to come down for dinner. Perhaps I had embarrassed her when I left her naked and alone outside, but I told myself it was for the best. Nothing good would come from starting something with the boss's daughter. And the General was my boss at the moment. I couldn't forget that even thinking about Avery sexually was disrespecting someone who had done a lot for me.

When I'd gone for my run-slash-perimeter check at two-thirty that morning, the light had been on in the attic, so I knew Avery had been up late, but it was past midday now, and she hadn't made her daily trip to the coffeepot yet.

It was time for an olive branch.

Pulling her favorite mug out of the cupboard, I fixed her coffee the way she liked it, grimacing as I half-and-half-ed the coffee and creamer in the cup. With a generous squeeze of caramel syrup on top to finish off the sugary nightmare, I wandered upstairs with mug in hand to search out my charge. Her bedroom was empty, sheets a messy pile on top of her mattress. No rush of water came from her bathroom, so I continued up the next flight of stairs to the attic.

The silence as I ascended to the top floor of the house made the hairs stand up on the back of my neck. Avery seemed to prefer different genres of music, depending on what project she was working on. Blues, country, classical; I'd heard all of them at different times of the day. But there was always something playing up here. Pushing open the door, I stepped into the empty workroom.

"Avery?"

The painting beside the window gave me nothing. The swirl of colors and vaguely humanoid face seeming to leer at me, condemning my presence in her personal space. Retracing my steps, I systematically worked through each room on the second floor, stubbornly tamping down the anxiety crawling through me as each door opened into yet another Avery-free room. A heavy wooden set of double doors loomed at the end of the hall, the ornate carving giving me pause. It seemed like the kind of room where secrets were held.

Fuck it, finding Avery was more important than whatever might be hidden in there.

I pushed the doors open and came face to face with rows and rows of books. A library, Christ. Navigating between the rows of shelves, I came to a clear space flushed with sunlight. A sitting area with high-backed, plush chairs took up the majority of the space in front of a window with a bench built in beneath it.

I let out a heavy breath.

In one corner of the bench, curled up in a pile of cushions with one foot hanging over the edge, was Avery. Fast asleep. As though she were a magnet and I were just a hunk of metal, I was drawn across the space between us until I stood over her, watching her in sleep like a goddamn creeper.

Her brow furrowed, and I couldn't help but try to smooth the lines away with a thumb. Her head turned into my touch, as though even in sleep she couldn't get close enough. She deserved better than what I, or even the General, could give her.

The thought hit me hard, and I quickly snatched my hand away. She had been right the other day when she'd called me destructive. I was responsible for the undoing of so much, and even if I had tried to make things right, I'd given up. Run away when things got hard.

I refused to do that again.

Avery sighed, her eyelids fluttering before opening; her sleepy hazel stare latching onto me.

"Good morning," she muttered, stretching her legs out and not bothering to stifle a yawn.

"Hardly morning. What are you doing in here?"

I offered her the cup of coffee I had carted all over the house in my search for her. She accepted the mug with a grin, taking a long draw of the caffeine before refocusing on me.

"I came down here this morning. I must have fallen asleep. It's really nice in the sun here. You should try it."

I grunted, lifting her feet and sliding onto the bench next to her. Needing something to do with my hands, I started working the muscles in her feet. Kneading and massaging while trying to convince myself it wasn't because I was still processing the anxiety of not being able to find her. We sat quietly for a while, Avery sipping her coffee and periodically groaning when I hit a particularly tender spot on her feet.

"I'm sorry," I blurted. Shit, I hadn't meant to say that.

"For what?" she asked, wiggling her feet to get me to continue massaging when I paused.

"I shouldn't have messed with you like that yesterday. I made you uncomfortable. So, yeah. I'm sorry." Eloquent as a rock, as always.

"Which part are you apologizing for?"

"The... Well, all of it, really."

She cocked her head, eyeing me far closer than I wanted her to. Her father may have thought she was a brat and a flake, but there was a hell of a lot more to her that I couldn't afford to explore.

"From my perspective, the only discomfort came from you working me up and not following through. Is cold feet a common thing for you, Logan? A little performance anxiety, maybe?"

I revised my previous thought. Brat was most definitely a fitting descriptor.

"Look, I don't pursue men who are genuinely not interested in me. I think we could work really well together, so tell me. Do you want me, Logan?"

"Yes. No. Fuck, I can't want you. I'm here to keep you safe."

"I can keep myself safe. But to be clear, you're saying keeping me safe and fucking me are mutually exclusive? It would seem the best way to keep an eye on me would be to share my bed."

I surged to my feet in agitation. How was I supposed to argue with that logic? I could spout some bullshit about respect for her father, or not wanting her, but when it came down to it... No, I couldn't do this. Avery's hand shot out, wrapping around my wrist as I took a step away from her.

"Tell me right now that you have no interest in me, and I'll let you go. If you're doing this for some shitty bro code, white knight bullshit, I'm going to break you down and get behind those walls, because I think I can do as much for you as you can for me."

My jaw ticked as I tried to force out the words. *I don't like you. I'm not interested in you. My dominant side wants to tame you in ways that might scare you.*

Instead of voicing anything, I broke her grip and strode out.

Before I gave that smart mouth something else to do.

9

AVERY

*A*fter our showdown in the library, I took a long, hot shower and let off some steam, so to speak. If Logan didn't crack soon, I was going to end up with hand cramps.

I'd meant what I said to him in the library. If he'd said didn't want me, I'd let it go. Despite the heat that lurked in his gaze. And the fact he knew how I liked my coffee. He cared about me, even if he didn't want to admit it because of some misplaced loyalty to my father. I wasn't going to let that man take something that could be so good for me and Logan away from us.

I toweled off and pulled on a set of black pants and top, ready to work off some of the lingering sexual tension in a fighting scenario.

Scraping my hair off my neck as I trotted down the stairs, I ducked into the kitchen to fill my keep-cup with coffee before I headed out.

"Where are you going?" Logan asked, emerging from the back hall. For such a big guy, he moved like a ghost.

"Out. I'll be back in a couple of hours."

It wasn't so much that I distrusted Logan, but I knew anything I told him about my extracurricular activities would make it back to my father, who would either ridicule my chosen sport, or immediately insist I quit because fighting was "unbecoming of a woman."

Neither was acceptable, and both were an almost certainty. Besides, I enjoyed holding something back from Logan. He had all the power in this situation. He was *the protector*, looking after the General's good-for-nothing brat of a daughter. He was the one holding back from our mutual attraction. Deeper down there was also still that biting cut that he was the one my father had chosen to love. And fuck him for saying I had daddy issues.

"Avery—"

"See you!" I gave him a cheery wave and reached for the table I kept my car keys on.

"Where—?"

The jingle of keys wrenched my head back in Logan's direction.

"I'll drive."

"No."

"Then you're not going."

Taking a deep breath through my nose, I backtracked until I was standing toe to toe with the current bane of my existence.

"I have been driving myself places for almost a decade. You do not need to come in here and start dictating my life to me."

My heart pounded as he curled his body over mine. His breath tickled the shell of my ear as he thoroughly invaded my personal space.

"I thought you wanted me to take control." His hand collared my throat as he traced the tip of his nose down my cheek. "To put you on your knees and force you to take my cock like a good girl? You'd look so pretty all tied up with my handprints all over this ass."

His fingers danced up the back of my thigh, sliding over the skin-tight pants and hooking into the crease where leg met ass as he tightened the hand around my throat just enough to make swallowing difficult. Every fiber of my being wanted what he was saying, but the memory of him leaving me on the floor in the attic, and again by the pool, gave me the presence of mind to get out of his grasp.

"I never said I'd make it easy on you. Besides, relinquishing control in the bedroom is completely different to being a full-time sub. That's not my thing."

He nodded, stepping around me and bee-lining for the door.

"Good. I'm not interested in a full-time sub." He paused at the door, shooting a smirk over his shoulder.

"I'm still driving, though. Are you coming?"

I growled in frustration, but one glance at the clock told me I'd have to allow the chauffeur act, then ditch him at the mall. I still thought the bodyguard routine was an overreaction but had to admit it was nice having company, even if he did regularly drive me mad.

Throwing myself into the passenger seat, I rolled my eyes as Logan struggled for a moment with my sticky clutch before my baby roared to life.

"I didn't know you drive stick," Logan said, moving the gear shift smoothly into second.

I smirked at him, unable to pass on the easy in he'd given me.

"I've never had any complaints about how I ride a stick. I know all the tricks to make them purr."

Logan shook his head, glancing out the side window, but I didn't miss the quirk of his lips. Bastard knew I was hilarious.

"You can admit I'm funny, Logan. I promise I won't hold it against—Hey, that's a red light."

"I know," he grunted, pumping my unresponsive brake pedal to the chorus of hideous screeches from my brake pads.

Cars slowed around us as the light approached, but my little bug didn't seem to want to obey. If anything, the hill we were going down was causing an increase in speed.

"Logan..."

"I know." We shot through the red light and into the path of an eighteen-wheeler.

"Hold tight."

Switching pedals, Logan floored the gas, rocketing us out of the intersection to the cacophony of horns blaring before mounting the curb, down shifting gears, and throwing the car into a turn as he hauled on the parking brake. The car skidded, sending grass and dirt flying around us, and finally came to rest alongside a chain-link fence that looked like it had seen better days.

With the abrupt halt of our forward momentum, an eerie vacuum seemed to settle over us, sucking away the outside world until all that existed was Logan and me, our panting breaths deafening in the void.

It took a greater effort than I could have imagined to convince my shaking hand to release the death grip I had on the panic handle; but as it slipped free, I found the task of keeping it elevated beyond my capability. From a distance, I heard someone curse.

It was getting increasingly difficult to hear as the rushing sound of the ocean began to fill my ears. Odd. I hadn't thought we were close enough to hear the ocean, but the hissing grew louder and louder until I was forced to close my eyes against the onslaught of noise.

My body felt weightless for a moment, and I wondered if I were being swept out to sea. Dragged out beyond the horizon, where the waves could swallow me up and send me to the depths.

The squeeze of my jaw was the first indicator I wasn't about to drown. The next was something warm and moist pressing against my mouth.

Lips.

Someone was kissing me.

Awareness returned to me in a powerful rush that made me gasp. Logan took advantage, thrusting his tongue against mine, begging me to come back to him without words. With a moan, I fisted his shirt, returning the kiss with equal fervor. He was a man possessed, his arms crushing me to him as though he was anchoring me to this life. Maybe he was. I had no idea where I'd been a minute ago, but it hadn't been good.

With a growl, Logan pulled back. I whimpered, but he didn't go far. His hands ran over my hair, down my neck, and over my shoulders, checking for anything out of place. Any injury that needed tending.

Now I was more conscious, I realized I was sitting on the bonnet of my bug. Behind me, my passenger side door stood open, and opposite, the driver's side window had been cranked down, the door too close to the fence to be opened.

"I'm okay," I mumbled, surveying the yards of tire tracks from the road to the place we'd stopped. Grass and dirt were strewn about as though massacred with a chainsaw.

"Jesus, you scared me. What the hell happened?"

"I think the brakes failed."

Logan huffed, crooking a finger under my chin to raise my eyes to his. "I mean to you. I think you went into shock. We need to get you looked over by a doctor. Now."

It wasn't until Logan scooped me into his arms that I realized he had perched me on my car's hood to check me over.

"I can walk," I grumbled half-heartedly. It was probably a lie, but the more awareness returned, the more I felt the need to protest the manhandling.

He ignored me, typing one handed on his cell and cradling me to him as though I weighed nothing.

"Logan."

"Bear's going to swing by and take us to a doc he trusts. He's organizing a tow for us as well. I want that car checked out. There's no way those brakes should have failed without tampering."

"How would you know?"

He cocked a brow at me, his nose almost touching mine. Damn, he was close.

"You think I didn't check your car out before I let you drive it when I took this job? I take your safety seriously, hen. When are you going to get that through your head?"

"Because I'm a job, right?" I asked, my need for space from him winning out over any support I could have wanted from him.

He let me go reluctantly, keeping a hand close to my elbow as I leaned my ass against my car, pretending I was relaxing rather than using it to stay upright.

"Avery," he warned.

Exhaustion washed over me, and I gave into the urge to rest, letting my knees buckle until I sat sprawled on the grass.

"Forget it. I don't want to talk about that right now. In fact, why don't we wait for your friend in silence?"

Logan paced, watching me from the corner of his eye on each pass, until I was ready to scream. Eventually, he slid down beside me, leaning his head against the car door and silently slipping his fingers through mine.

Unable to resist the olive branch, I squeezed his fingers and laid my head back, watching fluffy wisps of clouds drift across the bright blue of the sky.

"You're really frustrating me with this hot and cold act, you know?" I blurted.

His fingers spasmed in my grip. I wasn't sure what made me call him on the game we seemed to be playing, blame it on concussion, or shock, or whatever, but in this moment, I needed him to drop the bullshit.

"You treat me like a burden, that I'm stupid for being attracted to you, and in the next breath, you're kissing me or looking at me like you want to devour me. We're both consenting adults, so what the hell?"

Logan sat silently for so long I was ready to scream. A car rumbled past, and I pictured myself running after it, flagging it down, and taking off, just to get away from this head fuck of a bodyguard of mine.

He sighed, the sound carrying with it burdens unspoken. "You couldn't—"

"Do not tell me I couldn't handle you. You have no idea what I'm capable of. Don't make assumptions, Logan. It makes an ass out of you and me."

In a move so fast my rattled mind could barely track it, he straddled my splayed legs, cupping my jaw in a strong hand and forcing my head back so I could see his huge body looming over me.

"You have no idea the things I want to do to you, Avery. I want to spank the fuck out of you for your bratty attitude. I want to tie you up and fuck every one of your holes until you're so lost in my possession that you can't speak. I want to push your boundaries; see you straddle the line of pleasure and pain. You'd take it so beautifully." He bent down until his cheek was pressed against mine. "I want to give you pleasure until you're boneless one day, then deny your completion until you're mad with need the next. You would be entirely mine."

I shuddered at the growl in his voice, my eyes sliding closed as I surrendered to his words. I wanted everything he was saying. More than I'd ever admit aloud.

A cool breeze danced through the space between us, and I snapped my eyes up to see Logan standing back a step.

"But I was hired to keep you safe, hen. I can't do that if I'm wrapped up in this thing you want us to start. Your father wouldn't approve of it, and he'd be right."

"Fuck my father."

"That's not my kink, but that might be between you and him. I'm going to keep doing my job."

Behind him, a black SUV mounted the curb, and a giant of a man stepped out. Logan was big, but this guy made him look like a grade schooler by comparison. The guy ran a hand through his tousled black hair and surveyed the scene before crossing to Logan and thumping his shoulder with a meaty paw.

"What the hell did you manage to do here?"

Logan shrugged off the hand, but immediately turned to give the guy a man hug.

"Brakes failed. Can your guy take a look and let me know if they've been tampered with?"

"Oh, yeah, the car looks like it's seen better days, but I was talking about what you did to piss her off."

He came to crouch in front of me, ignoring a warning growl from Logan. He had a ruggedly handsome face, with lines around the eyes that made me think he liked to smile. Dark eyes sparkled at me as he held out a hand.

"Pleased to meet you, ma'am, I'm Bear. It sounds like you've had one hell of a morning with this lughead over here."

The corner of my mouth twitched in response to his gentle smile.

"Avery. You're right. It has been a morning. Thank you for coming."

Bear tapped his fingers to his forehead in a facsimile of a salute and offered a hand. "I have wonderful, heated seats and brakes in working order."

I laughed, allowing him to pull me to my feet. Despite his size, Bear was the most non-threatening man I'd ever met. The fact he was Army meant he definitely had that darker side, but I was thankful for a buffer between Logan and me after our last conversation, and Bear was astute enough to provide that service.

Once we were settled in Bear's truck, with me in front despite Logan's protest, we waited for the tow truck to arrive and load up my poor car.

"We'll check it out and deliver it back to the house," the mechanic advised, tapping the side of Bear's truck in farewell before heading off.

"We need to go to the hospital," Logan announced from the back seat as Bear started the ignition.

"What for?" Bear asked, glancing in the rearview mirror, his brows furrowing.

"Avery's just been in an accident. We need to have her checked out."

"I'm fine."

Bear looked between me and the back seat.

"She doesn't look like she's hurt."

"I'm fine."

Logan was being unreasonable. It had been well over an hour since the accident, and although I'd felt loopy for the first half hour, the feeling had passed, and I'd been chatting with Bear easily while we waited for the tow.

I explained this to Logan with as much patience as I could muster. Bear reluctantly backed me up, suggesting we get some food.

We went to the hospital.

LOGAN

*I*t wasn't until the doc gave Avery the all-clear that I could take a full breath again.

Bear gave me a knowing smirk when the announcement came but blessedly left shit well enough alone.

This girl was getting under my skin in a way that terrified me. No one had ever affected me the way she did. Not even...

"Logan?"

"What?"

Avery huffed, her face slightly flushed as she tried and failed to suppress her irritation.

"He said I'm fine. Just like I told you I was. Can we go home now?"

The word hit me like a physical blow, and the farmhouse took up space front and center in my mind. Maybe when this was all over, when the renovations were done, and the threat detained, I could move her in with me. I'd already had vague plans of turning the second bedroom into a playroom...

Coughing the sudden tightness from my throat, I nodded toward the door.

No plans until the job is done, Tanner.

Avery grinned, sliding from the bed and sashaying her sassy ass out of the room.

Bear slapped me on the shoulder; a silent *you're a goner, man* written all over his face.

"Shut up," I grumbled, hurrying to get eyes back on Avery before she could get into any more trouble. The rumbling laugh that followed me out the door was not appreciated.

I was going to have to report in to General Walker when we returned to the house. The stalker activity was escalating, and I was going to have to reevaluate my security regime. This person was skilled. Experienced in a way that made me wonder if I was dealing with someone with a military background. Had the General pissed someone off somewhere along the way? Perhaps it had nothing to do with his current political aspirations and everything to do with a past grievance. Shit.

I mulled over everything I knew of the case so far, analyzing every detail to the point of paranoia. The slamming of a door broke me from my musings some immeasurable time later. Avery was halfway up the drive, waving at Bear. The woman had no sense of self preservation. Cursing, I threw myself out of Bear's truck after her, determined to get ahead of her and sweep the house so she wouldn't be jumped the second she got inside.

"Wait here," I muttered, pointing at the stoop and sliding past her into the house.

Systematically working through the house, I cleared each room thoroughly, especially the library on the second floor. After checking her attic hideaway, I jogged downstairs, ready to let her know things were safe, to find her sitting at the kitchen counter, coffee in hand, chatting with Luciana as she kneaded dough.

"Have you forgotten someone tried to kill you this morning? You were supposed to wait on the stoop."

Avery hid a grin behind her coffee cup as Luciana snorted. "It seemed a little exposed on the street. I'm more than safe with Luciana here, anyway. We're protecting each other while we chat, right?"

Luciana gave a sharp nod as she continued to work the dough.

Who knew protecting one woman would be a harder task than fighting the enemy on their own turf? Then again... maybe that was how I needed to start thinking of this assignment. It was sexual warfare, the likes of which I was loathe to admit I found intriguing. Whether it was genuine attraction, or a way to strike out at her father, Avery had decided I had a target on my back. She was gunning for me, and I was losing the will to resist the game. Fuck.

Rather than engage in the current battle, I excused myself to the General's office to submit a progress report.

"Any reason you called this check in three hours early, Tanner? Don't tell me my daughter is being difficult."

"Ah, no, Sir. We have had a possible escalation in the threat, though."

I explained the situation with Avery's car and my suspicions regarding tampering. I began a report on Avery's medical condition only to be cut off by the General.

"Have there been any other incursions onto my property? Any sign of breaches on the house?"

"No, sir. Avery's car has been parked on the street outside of the fence line. All cameras are present and in working order. I've had no indication the individual has been closer than the front gate. We have no footage of anyone tampering with the car, but the mechanics are calling as soon as they have a definitive explanation for the brake failure."

A soft click diverted my attention from the General's reply. Avery stood with her back against the door, a smirk on her face warning her bratty side was out to play.

Eyes locked on mine, she crossed her hands at her front, gripping the hem of her t-shirt and whipping it over her head in a smooth move, revealing a tight black sports bra. The zip at the front had slipped throughout the day, revealing a mouth-watering glimpse of cleavage. I wanted to bury my face in it.

Avery smirked, as though reading my mind, and shimmied her pants down over her hips, stepping out of the fabric as she sauntered across the room.

"Yes, sir," I muttered in response to the upward inflection I heard on whatever the General had just asked.

"Are you listening, Tanner?" The General's whip-like voice tore my attention back to the computer screen in front of me as Avery sank to her knees and crawled under the desk.

"Sorry, Sir. Just, ah... distracted."

"I can't afford to have you distracted. Get your head in the game, son."

A thump and a muffled curse came from below the desk. My little hen had grown tired of waiting, it seemed.

"My head's where it needs to be, Sir. I assure you."

At least... it was about to be. My dick stiffened as a small hand wrapped around my ankle. Shit. I should have put an end to the call and punished Avery for being so presumptuous, but the thought of her lips... Hell, the idea of her sucking me off while her father spoke to me, completely oblivious, was too tempting to resist.

"I'm investigating a couple of possible leads on the identity of the stalker, and I'm expecting a sitrep from the mechanics any minute."

Out of sight of the camera, Avery moved in between my knees and ran both hands up the inside of my thighs. Her thumbs brushed over my balls and up the length of my twitching erection.

Fucking tease.

Nodding in agreement to whatever the General was demanding, I tangled a hand through her hair and pulled her face tight against my crotch, smothering her for a long minute. When I let her breathe, she didn't move her face right away, opting instead to graze her teeth over my sack. She was going to do that again on bare skin. I'd make sure of it. Without breaking eye contact with her father on the screen, I gripped her chin tightly with one hand and worked my zipper with the other, freeing myself and guiding her face toward my tip.

"There's no margin for error here, Tanner. The campaign is about to start, and I don't want to see anything in the media about my fuckup of a daughter."

The suckling on my head paused, and without giving her time to overthink what her father had said, I thrust into her mouth so deep I felt her gag. Fuck, that felt good.

"She's been well behaved so far, Sir," I said, stroking her cheek as she pulled back, a string of saliva connecting us before she moved back over me. "A very good girl. She's handling this all quite well, considering."

Her nose brushed my stomach, and I held her in place just long enough to feel her squirm under my hand.

"Keep an eye on her. She's her mother's daughter, and I'd hate to see something bad happen to her."

The words were innocuous, but the tone sent warning bells through the back of my brain. Avery fisted my cock, licking my balls into her mouth and sucking them like candy.

Shit, I needed to end this before I nutted in front of my boss and gave all the power to this brat.

"Will do, Sir. There's a call coming through from the mechanics now. I'll update you as soon as there's more intel."

The General agreed, and I barely got through our farewells and signed off before I reached under the desk and hauled Avery over it.

Flattening myself against her near-naked body, I growled in her ear. "You think it's funny to get me worked up in front of your father? Trying to top from the bottom, hen? I've got some bad news for you. You're getting your wish." I thrust my cock against her panty-covered ass, enjoying her moan of pleasure for a moment before snapping into dominant mode.

"We're going to play now. If we're in a scene and you're uncomfortable with anything, say yellow, and we'll switch gears. You say red and the game stops. Immediately. If I think you're using yellow to control me, I'll call red, and we won't play again that day. Understand?"

"Yes," she hissed, grinding her ass into my erection.

I pulled off her and palmed her ass in both hands.

Running my fingers under the seams of her panties, I pulled them up until they were wedged into her ass crack. The fabric pressed tight against her pussy lips, and both ass cheeks were bared for me.

Crack.

I brought my hand down on her left ass cheek and repeated it on her right. She gasped and moaned at the first contact, her breath quickly becoming labored as I fell into a rhythm until both globes glowed red from my handprints. Dropping to my knees, I gripped her reddened skin and spread her ass cheeks wide, burying my nose in her pussy. Unable to resist a taste, I ran my tongue all the way from clit to asshole just once before I straightened and pulled her panties back into place.

"What...?" Her voice was rough, her eyes dazed as she looked over her shoulder in confusion.

"Bad girls don't get to come. Now I know what your pussy smells like. If you finish yourself off, I'll know, and you won't like the consequences."

I gripped her fingers to make my meaning clear and waited for the realization that she wasn't getting fucked to set in. Sure enough, her face clouded over with the tantrum I had expected. However, in the next moment, it was gone. A sly smile stretched across her face.

"Okay, Daddy. I'll be a good girl and not use my fingers to come."

"I'm not your father." But fuck, hearing the name pass those lips was sinfully arousing.

"No. You're not. But you were right about one thing. I do have daddy issues, because you're fucking with my head. I think the nickname is fitting."

I didn't miss the way her knees threatened to buckle as she straightened, even as she tried to shrug off her statement. I let her get to the door, watching each step land a little faster than the one before. As she pulled the wooden slab wide, ready to make her escape, I stopped her.

"No using the vibrator I know you have stashed upstairs, either."

The slew of curse words was cut off as she slammed the door, and I allowed my smirk to become a full-blown grin, sinking back into the chair I had previously occupied. Tucking my still-hard dick into my pants, I didn't even care that I hadn't finished. I'd take care of it later.

The satisfaction of punishing Avery—of knowing she would adhere to the punishment despite her tantrum—was far more rewarding to me. It showed me we could work together. For the first time, I entertained the idea that things could work out between Avery and me.

A buzzing broke through my thoughts. Reaching for my ringing cell, a flash of silver below the desk caught my eye. A key. I picked it up and inspected it, connecting the call absently.

"Hey, Bear."

"Hey, man. I just got off the phone from the mechanics. What the fuck are you mixed up in? The guys said it looked like her brake pads had been hacked apart, and her brake lines were riddled with holes. No way this wasn't sabotage."

I grunted, drumming the key on the desk in thought. It wasn't a great surprise that Avery's car had been sabotaged. Bear's voice was full of concern for me, and I could hear his unspoken request for me to lose the job and keep myself safe. Bear had never been a great fan of the General, not that he'd said anything aloud, but I'd seen it in his expression when the General spoke about women, in the way he often left the room at the moment the General entered.

Bear was a pacifist at heart, the only thing making him suited for a life in the military his size.

I knew he wanted me to leave, but the only thing that made my blood run cold, the thing that would keep me up at night, was the thought of what could have happened if I hadn't insisted on driving her today.

Avery's death was an unacceptable outcome on this mission. The problem was that I was becoming increasingly concerned that the reasoning behind it had little to do with her father and everything to do with who she was becoming to me.

11

AVERY

I was in a bitch of a mood. My blood ran too hot, and I couldn't focus on anything past the throbbing of my ass and the corresponding pulse in my clit.

Who the hell was Logan Tanner to get me so worked up and refuse to finish me off?

I thought we were finally past the hot and cold routine. The sensation of being held by the hair, the inability to breathe as he'd held me tightly against his crotch. I could still taste the precum on the back of my tongue. It had been perfect, right down to the way he'd choked me with his cock. I wanted him to do it again. Maybe tied up next time.

I rolled onto my back, my bedspread crinkling beneath me, and tiptoed my fingers down my stomach to tease the top of my panties. I hadn't bothered to put clothes on after our encounter. If he wanted to hold out, I'd do everything in my power to make him crack open.

Screw it. Feeling undeniably naughty, and somewhat hoping I would get caught in the act, I slid a hand inside the waistband of my panties. I was so worked up, I could get it done and jump straight into the shower before Logan left my father's office. Sliding my fingers over soft curls, I paused at the top of my slit.

A loud rumbling on my nightstand made me rip my hand away guiltily, and I stared at my cell in confusion for a long second. Did he know? Was he calling to reprimand me? With a shaking hand, I retrieved my cell and accepted the call with the unknown caller ID.

"Hello?"

There was a subtle click, and then the sound of breathing. Sitting up, I re-checked the caller ID to confirm it was still an unknown number.

"Hello?"

Another couple of heartbeats of silence before a voice I'd know anywhere whispered, "Avery."

"Mom!"

When nothing by silence came back, I checked to see the call had ended.

Ten years. Not a word for ten years, and she calls the same day I have an inexplicable car accident?

Pulling up my recent calls, I confirmed the number hadn't miraculously appeared and jumped up to pace.

Why make contact now?

A Google search turned up exactly the same shit it had every other time I had looked for her in the last decade. Namely, nothing. She was a ghost. I hadn't understood it when she first left, but as I got older, it made sense that the only way to escape my father's influence would be to disappear off the face of the earth.

I glanced at the door, slowing to a stop as an idea formed. Logan was connected. He knew as many tech savvy people as my father. Maybe he could trace the call.

Taking the stairs two at a time, I skidded on the floorboards as I raced down the hall toward my father's office. Flinging open the door, I found Logan sitting in the same chair I'd left him, talking on his cell in a low voice.

"You're sure? A woman? I swear, none of this makes any damn sense. Hang on, Avery just came in. I'll put you on speaker. Uh huh. Yeah, she deserves to know. Yup. Hang on."

Waving me closer, he laid his cell flat on the desk and pushed a button.

"She can hear you now. Say hello, Avery."

"Hi?"

"Hi, Avery, I was just telling Logan the red motorcycle that's been following you is owned by a woman. A Lorna Marshall. Description is five-foot-four, blonde hair, hazel eyes. Date of birth March eighteenth, nineteen seventy-two. The name could be an alias, but just in case it isn't, is any of that familiar to you?"

A ringing started in my ears, pulling at the back of my eyeballs in a way that made me worry my head could cave in.

"Avery?" Logan's voice was softer than I'd ever heard it. "Hen, sit down. You look like you're about to hit the deck. Damon, I'll call you back. Thanks, man."

Warm arms wrapped around me, and I felt weightless. The place where my face pressed against warm flesh under fabric was the only thing grounding me. I inhaled deeply, the scent of leather and bourbon so uniquely him, I could have cried.

"Maybe I should get a second consult from the doctor," he muttered, settling me on his lap.

The tingling receded from my fingers, and I took a moment to breathe before straightening to look into Logan's worried eyes.

"I'm sorry. I didn't mean to scare you like that. I'm fine.... Well, maybe fine as an acronym? You know... fucked up, insecure, neurotic, and emotional?" I huffed a half-hearted laugh, but clearly Logan wasn't interested in dark humor at that moment.

"What just happened?" he asked, his hands tightening on me subtly.

"So... I came down here with a suspicion, and then that guy pretty much cemented it. But I don't know how it's possible, and why now, because it doesn't really make sense... you know?"

"I'm going to need a noun here, hen," Logan said with the slightest lift of his lips.

"Right. Sorry." I huffed a laugh.

"I just received a phone call from a private number. The caller said my name, and I'd swear it was my mother's voice. Then the woman that guy just described... it's her. I haven't seen her in a decade. I've looked for her. My father has looked for her. Neither of us ever found anything. And now she turns up and things start going wrong? What's her motive? Why me?"

A soothing weight settled on my head and slid down my hair until it reached the center of my back and lifted. It resettled on my head and repeated the motion in a slow stroke that made me want to close my eyes against the world and sleep. Giving in to the impulse, I dropped my head to his collarbone and listened to him breathe as he thought through what I'd told him.

The subtle tick of my father's Thomas Tompion clock was the only sound in the room, making it easy to focus on the vitality of the man beneath me. The thump of his heart, the whoosh of his breath. Our encounter in this office less than an hour ago now seemed like a lifetime away. Had it happened? Or had my vivid imagination invaded an impromptu nap I was unaware of taking?

I hated to admit how desperately I wanted Logan to want me, because then I'd also have to acknowledge how painfully lonely I had become. It wasn't entirely about companionship, though. Logan called to a part of me that had been buried for years. A part that wanted to be safe enough to let go. I trusted Logan.

Shit.

"Are you all right?" His deep voice vibrated through my head where it lay on his chest.

"I don't know," I answered honestly.

Logan hummed.

"I think there's only one important thing we need right now. Do you feel up to making a life-changing decision?"

I sat up, enjoying the way his hands tightened to keep me from leaving. His sherry eyes were wide, his ball cap sitting slightly askew on his head.

"What decision?"

"Chocolate? Or vanilla?"

A grin broke across my face, turning into a shrieking laugh as he stood, keeping me firmly in his arms. Swiping the cap from his head, I propped it over my own hair, backward.

"Dude, I'm anything but vanilla. I thought you'd have worked that out while I was gagging on your dick before."

Logan's eyes narrowed, but I didn't miss the twitch in his cheek.

"Don't make me spank you again, hen."

I was going to enjoy being his brat.

ARMED WITH A SPOON EACH, WE TOOK OUR MEAL IN the media room, the closest thing we had to a comfortable room on the premises. Logan offered me the first scoop of the tub of chocolate fudge ice cream we'd brought with us.

"If you weren't here with me, having car accidents and generally holding me captive on my father's orders, what would you be doing?" I asked, licking the bottom of my spoon before sucking the ice cream into my mouth.

He watched closely, eyes tracking every lick as his spoon hovered above the ice cream tub, forgotten mid-strike.

Taking advantage of his distraction, I leaned over and stole the next scoop with a grin. Logan caught my wrist and guided the laden spoon to his mouth, eyes locked on mine until he'd sucked it clean. Damn, that was hot.

Scooping his own spoonful, he offered the tub to me once he was good and ready.

"Renovating my farmhouse. That was my plan before this, and it'll be my plan once we know you're safe. How about you? Any people you should be seeing? Places to go? You still haven't told me where you ran off to the other day."

He had no idea what he was asking.

"I have one place I can go that's mine. I would continue going there. Otherwise, my life wouldn't be much different. You just wouldn't be here."

Logan frowned, his brows darkening despite the fact I still wore his cap.

"You don't have friends you'd be hanging out with? I thought I'd have supervised at least one playdate by now."

"I don't have any friends."

Logan chuckled but cut the noise short as he realized I was dead serious.

I didn't want to talk about this... did I? Family secrets were kept locked up for a reason, but staring into the nonjudgmental gaze before me, the knowledge burned in my throat.

"Every girlfriend I've had since my mom left has ended up in my dad's bed."

"What—"

"He fucks them. It's some messed up game for him. I get close to someone, and if they're male, he scares them off, pretending it's to preserve my honor or some shit. If it's a female, he seduces them. The last female friend I had is currently in Washington, servicing my father. Hell, for all I know, she was under his desk while I was under yours."

The laugh that left my throat was bitter enough to burn, and the mouthful of ice cream I'd eaten churned in my gut. The look on Logan's face was worse as he did the math I'd half hoped, half dreaded he'd make.

"Weren't you fifteen when your mother left?"

Logan loved my father. Everyone did. I knew he wouldn't have agreed to this screwy arrangement otherwise. Still, I couldn't keep the truth from him.

"Yeah. I was."

God, I couldn't do this.

Surging to my feet, I gave him a tight smile and excused myself. I didn't have a plan except to get out from under the eyes of the man who had just had the curtain pulled back on someone he'd idolized. I didn't want to see the break that occurred when reality hit them. Or even worse, the mental gymnastics some people pulled to maintain the status quo.

The first time it had happened, it had been during a sleepover at our house. Samantha had been her name. I had woken in the night and found her missing from her bed. In the morning, she had strutted into my room and proudly announced she was no longer a virgin. When she refused to report it to anyone, I took it to my homeroom teacher, who gave me a week's detention and a half-hour lecture on the damage rumors could cause to the reputation of others. Over the years, I'd been called petty, ignorant, and jealous more times than I cared to admit. Not once had anyone seen how wrong his behavior was.

A hand hooked around my elbow and momentum swung me into a hard chest I was getting to know quite well. Resisting the urge to seek comfort in it, I pushed away, only to have an arm wrap around my lower back, pinning me in place.

"I'm sorry he put you through that. It was a really shitty thing to do."

I heard each word individually, but my brain was having trouble processing the sentence as a whole.

"What...?"

"He abused his power and isolated you when he should have been someone you could trust. In case you don't already know this, it wasn't your fault."

"What...?" The next breath I took hitched as my vision blurred.

"Avery. Hen. It wasn't your fault."

A sob broke out of the depths of my chest, and I turned, ashamed of the emotional display. Logan turned me back into him and held me close, returning to the rhythmic stroking he had given me earlier.

"I had to protect them," I whimpered through my tears.

"I know, hen." He kept his voice low and soothing, never flinching in the face of my complete undoing.

As my sobs subsided, Logan stiffened and pulled me away carefully.

"Hen, I'm sorry, but I have to ask. Did he ever...?" The question hung between us; the fear of my answer not quite hidden in his eyes.

"No," I said, and the way his body relaxed made me want to hide the rest of the answer, but I'd started, and I found the words wouldn't stay put.

"But he had friends who tried. After Luciana saved me from the first creep, I started Kung Fu. That's where I went the other day. I train a few times a week and help with kids' classes."

"So that's how you managed to nail me in the nuts that day."

I laughed. I couldn't help it. The image of him bent over, struggling to breathe because he'd tackled me, was the most validating experience I'd had in a while.

"We fight to win, even if it means fighting dirty."

Logan snorted. "Yeah, well, I'd much prefer you treated them like you did today, in any case."

He cupped my jaw, using a thumb to swipe a stray tear from my cheek.

"I prefer that too," I said softly.

"Do you want some more ice cream? It's probably melting by now." Logan turned back toward the media room, and a wicked idea of exactly what he could do with that ice cream flashed through my head. On the heels of it flashed the pain of the last few minutes, and my libido threw its hands up in surrender.

"I actually think I might try to have an early night," I said, hooking a thumb over my shoulder at the last rays of the sun disappearing on the horizon.

"No problem," he said, smiling softly. I watched his ass as he strode back into the media room before turning and making my way upstairs, feeling lighter than I had in years.

Rather than going to bed, because despite what I said, I wouldn't be ready for sleep for hours to come, I headed up to my studio. After considering several possible projects, I settled down with charcoal and a blank piece of paper.

Tonight was a night for sketching.

12

LOGAN

"*P*lease, sir." *Her whimper drove me harder as I pounded into her, one ear cocked to sounds outside the utility tent we'd snuck into. Leaning over her back, I wrapped a hand around her mouth to smother the noises she couldn't suppress. It was risky having a midnight rendezvous while deployed, but Lana had always been a wild one, and things had been quiet lately. The enemy had been few and far between for the last week, and everyone was on edge.*

Especially Lana right now.

Shifting my hand higher, I ensured her nose was also covered and felt her pussy tighten around me with excitement as she tried and failed to suck air into her lungs. We couldn't play properly out here, but I'd make do where I could.

Her pulse was visible at the side of her throat, and I altered my pace to match it, releasing her mouth and allowing her one full breath before I wrapped her hair around my fist and wrenched her head back until she could look me in the eye.

I lifted a brow, slowing my strokes to a rolling pace that would keep her on edge without giving her the finish she was so desperate for. Tears ran down both cheeks, and she gave me a beautiful smile.

Perfect.

Pushing in as far as I could go, I wrenched her head back even farther, enjoying the curve of her spine, then reached around her body and pinched her clit hard.

I slammed my hand over her mouth just in time, absorbing her scream as she tightened around me so brutally that I couldn't help but follow her over the edge. Pulling out, I whipped off the condom and pumped my release all over her ass and pussy.We panted in the afterglow, our breaths loud in the quiet of the sleeping camp. I'd paid off the duty security team leader to look the other way just in case, but Lana didn't know that. The risk was half the fun.

"I suppose I should shower and get some sleep," she said, her voice brimming with reluctance.

I chuckled, sliding her panties back up over her hips and cupping her pussy over them. "You're not showering. You're going to sleep with my cum all over you like the dirty slut you are. Tomorrow morning, you'll report to me and ask permission to use the ablutions on your knees."

Lana's breath caught. She'd always had a slight degradation kink, and although it wasn't something that turned me on, I was happy to cater to her needs.

"Yes, Sir," she breathed, sliding her pants into place and buckling them as she moved toward the tent entrance.

"Avery," I called, and frowned. No, not Avery. Lana.

The raven-haired beauty turned, a dazzling smile on her face.

"Yes, Sir?" Her eyes weren't black, though. They were hazel. Her skin a porcelain that Lana's had never been. This wasn't right.

"Don't leave the tent," I whispered. But the words didn't carry, because that wasn't how things had gone.

Avery chuckled, flipping her pale blonde hair as she pulled back the flap on the tent.

A fireball billowed in through the opening, eviscerating my lover as I was thrown headfirst into a storage container. Everything went white.

"Logan!"

I threw myself toward the voice, half asleep and violent with panic after witnessing the death of someone who had been my responsibility. Landing hard, a soft body beneath me, I curled over it as though able to protect it from the fireball that was still vividly blooming in my mind.

"Logan," the voice called my name a second time, and I felt the cool brush of a hand over my heated skin.

Slowly, the dream receded, and I became aware that I was lying on the floor on top of Avery. When had she come down here?

I cursed, rolling away as it occurred to me that I was crushing her. She came with me, her arms wrapped tightly around my body until I was the one playing mattress. When she showed no signs of letting up, I returned the embrace slowly, allowing myself the space to breathe in her scent. Feel her whole and safe in my arms.

As my pulse returned to normal, and the sweat cooled on my skin, she pulled back enough to look me in the eye.

"Wanna talk about it?"

"Not really, but I probably should," I said, sitting up slowly and adjusting us so my back was against the sofa, and she was straddling my lap. Her core was warm against my lap, and I felt my dick sit up and take notice, but now was not the time.

Scrubbing a hand over my hair, I found the scar on the back of my skull from that night. Grasping her fingers, I guided them to the line of misshapen flesh I hid with my ball cap. My hair had grown out enough to hide it, but the paranoid part of my brain insisted I keep it covered, just in case. In case what? Fuck knew. Trauma was fun.

Avery's brow pulled low as she traced back and forth over my skin in gentle strokes.

"The night this happened, someone died. Well... more than one person, but one person's death was my fault." Christ. I'd never said the words aloud. Not even the Army shrink knew I held myself fully accountable for Lana's death. But I did, and I was.

Instead of protesting or interrupting, Avery nodded and waited patiently while I found the words.

"Lana and I... we had a casual thing. Not a relationship; more of a mutual exploration of kink and Dom/sub dynamics. Lana was an experienced sub and taught me a lot about the lifestyle.

I liked her. Anyway, we were deployed together. Middle of nowhere, and it had been quiet for long enough that we were all edgy. Your father was keeping everyone in line and insisting we hold position, even though there was buzz about us receiving orders to move out. Anyway, we snuck out one night to see each other. Take the edge off and... shit." My eyes burned as my throat tightened to the point of suffocation.

Wordlessly, Avery leaned in, pressing feather-light kisses over the side of my face and down my neck. Each kiss drawing a little of the tension from my throat. She lifted her head to check on me, but I didn't want to see the sympathy there. Fisting her hair, I pushed her face back to my skin, and she took the hint, working her way over my collarbone and down onto my chest.

As she swirled her tongue around one nipple, I dropped my head back and spoke to the ceiling.

"She was leaving the tent. Distracted from being freshly fucked. She walked straight into a fireball."

Avery hummed against my skin, leaving wet kisses as she moved to my other nipple.

"The enemy had taken over the camp while we slept. The security team were all killed, and explosives set around our supply tents."

Her mouth moved lower, licking over my abs, and she dipped her tongue into my navel. My hips lifted eagerly, the memory of her mouth almost enough to chase away the images of my dream.

"That night haunts me. Steals my sleep. But tonight, the dream changed."

Fingers hooked into the waistband of the basketball shorts I had been sleeping in, and she folded them down, releasing my erection.

"Avery, it was you. In my dream, I watched you get destroyed by the fire. You didn't stand a chance. I couldn't protect you." My voice sounded weak to my own ears. Lost. I hated the uncertainty I felt.

"I'm right here," she said, mouth brushing over my aching head. Locking eyes with me, she made sure I watched as she took me deep into her mouth.

Any other time, I would punish her severely for taking charge, but in this moment, the warmth of her mouth was the grounding I needed. As she worked her tongue over me, groaning in pleasure, I found the words came more easily by the minute.

"The way they were able to take over camp. Something wasn't right. They had to have received intel about our position. I tried to look into it after I was released from hospital but the trail ran cold. Have you ever known something with absolute certainty, but been unable to find the proof? Or even known what exactly you were looking for?"

Avery hummed, and jolts of arousal spiked along my spine. Fuck, she felt good.

"I looked until I felt like I was going mad. No one else thought it was weird. I even asked Damon to look into it. Your father told me it was PTSD, but..." I shook my head in frustration.

"Fuck, Avery. I need you," I groaned, pulling her off my cock.

"Yes," she hissed, letting her knees fall wide as I laid her on the floor and crawled on top of her. Cupping her pussy through her shorts, I found the fabric soaked.

"I might have a tiny oral fixation," she murmured, avoiding my eyes. "Like, not every day, but in the bedroom..."

I grabbed her jaw, forcing her gaze back to mine. "I can work with that," I said, letting a wolfish grin spread over my face.

This was going to be fun. I made a mental note to print a kink list out and go over her limits. Shit, I should have done that before our encounter in the library before. I cared about her safety, and rule number one was open communication before play. For tonight, I'd keep things vanilla, but tomorrow, we would be setting limits and discussing anything she wanted to explore.

"Get naked," I breathed in her ear, sitting back on my knees as she whipped off her t-shirt and shorts. I touched the curls between her legs, feeling the dewy softness stick to my fingertips as I ran them lightly over her mound.

"I want to wax this for you sometime soon," I murmured. Her breath hitched. "Would you like that?"

"I've never waxed before. Does it hurt?"

I smirked, thinking of the times I'd done it for Lana. She'd always told me it was the perfect tool to use on a masochist. The burn of the wax, the pain of the hair removal, and the fact that sex wasn't advised for twenty-four hours after the fact. Perfect for edging.

"We'll talk about it tomorrow. For now, I want to be inside you."

Avery groaned, opening her legs wider. Her pussy was flushed a beautiful deep pink, weeping with her arousal. Running two fingers up her slit, I circled her clit gently before diving down and pushing roughly into her opening. I pumped into her a few times, enjoying the way she squirmed on the floor, before scraping my fingertips along her g-spot and surging up over her.

"Open," I commanded, holding my soaking fingers to her lips.

She obeyed quickly, moaning as I pushed my fingers deep.

"Suck."

I positioned myself at her entrance and surged into her as she drew hard on my fingers, swirling her tongue around and in between the digits as though she couldn't get enough of her own taste. The dual sensation of her warm mouth and gripping cunt made my mind fog. Electric pulses lit up at the base of my spine.

Pulling my fingers from her mouth, I replaced them with my tongue, delving past her lips in search of the taste she had relished. Her desperate whimpers drove me on.

Why had I resisted this? She was right there with me, stroke for stroke, taking all I had to give and eager for more. Hitching her right leg over my shoulder, I rose to my knees, twisting her body and pulling her onto my cock at a new angle. She howled.

"Logan, yes!"

"Fuck you feel so good, hen. You're taking my cock so well."

She mewled, reaching down to rub at her clit. I slapped her hand away.

"Naughty girl. I'll decide when you come."

She growled, the cutest pout forming on her lips.

My thoughts screeched to a halt as I realized why everything was so slippery and perfect. Shit. Condom. This woman was going to ruin me. Never, in my entire sexual experience, had I forgotten to suit up.

Rearing back, I slumped against the sofa.

"What...?" Avery looked around in confusion.

"Come here, hen," I said softly, holding out a hand.

She came to me immediately, a question in her eyes.

"You're going to kneel over my face on the sofa." She nodded quickly, raising a leg, but I stopped her with a hand.

"Face outward."

She nodded again, swiveling until she kneeled precariously on the edge of the sofa, her pussy inches from my nose.

"Do you trust me, hen?"

"Yes."

"Put your weight on my arms. I'm going to fuck your face while I eat this juicy pussy."

Her responsiveness was such a turn on. Without hesitation, she leaned forward until my hands cupped the front of her shoulders. Splaying my legs wide, I lowered her until her mouth engulfed my dick. I wished I'd tied her hands before we started this, but she seemed content to hold them behind her back of her own accord.

I moved her over my dick, enjoying the burn in my shoulders at holding her weight. Once I found the right positioning and settled into a nice rough pace, I wrapped my lips around her labia and sucked hard, using just enough teeth to make her flinch. Fuck, she tasted amazing, and I felt my dick harden against her tongue as she retaliated with the barest scrape of her own teeth. Brat.

I worked my tongue around her pussy, plunging into her channel just to feel the squeeze and avoiding the one place she desperately wanted me.

Many women I'd been with had fallen into the habit of only seeking clitoral stimulation for orgasm, and I would use it if I had to, but I had the feeling Avery was capable of more. Fucking her a few more times with my tongue while I thrust my hips up, hitting the back of her throat, I moved higher up, massaging her perineum with undulating strokes. The sensation made her gasp, and I didn't miss the way her hips dropped subtly. She may not even have been conscious of it, but I moved farther still, circling around her asshole with firm strokes.

She choked out a cry, her voice muffled by my cock, and I pushed up hard enough to smother her with my balls.

I wanted to explore more, but my lower back was cramping with the need to come so, balancing her weight on one hand, I pushed three fingers into her pussy as I continued my assault on her sensitive skin and held her still as she screamed. As soon as she took a breath, I shifted my grip again and mercilessly fucked her face until I spilled down her throat.

She swallowed every drop, taking her weight on her hands and cleaning my dick with long strokes of her tongue that prolonged the aftershocks running through my body. As she slid down my body and tried to stand on shaky legs, I pulled her back to me, cradling her in my lap and taking a moment to breathe.

"We didn't have a condom." I felt the need to explain.

Avery chuckled. "I'm not sorry. I mean, I'm on birth control, so it wouldn't have mattered, but that was the most intense orgasm I've ever had in my life, so I'm not sorry."

I hummed in relief and lay my head on top of hers. We sat quietly for a few minutes, then crawled onto the sofa and fell asleep in a tangle of satisfied limbs.

13

AVERY

*M*y body was still humming the next morning when I woke, unbearably hot, with male limbs wrapped so tightly around me I couldn't move.

"Logan," I whispered, nudging him with a shoulder and suppressing a grin when all he did was tighten his grip on me.

I'd never seen him sleep so late. We'd always been on this alternating schedule where he slept the first half of the night, and I the second. Wriggling around until I could see his face, I took a moment to appreciate the way it relaxed in sleep. He always seemed so tense. Either scowling or smirking, he had walls almost as tall as my own.

Except last night.

I'd come downstairs for a glass of water when I heard him shouting in his sleep. What he'd told me... I couldn't imagine going through that. And to have no answers for how it happened? It would kill me. I hadn't expected him to share so much with me, and in the light of day, the vulnerability he'd shown, compared with the wicked things we'd done, made me squirm. I wanted to do it again. I wanted more.

If he considered last night vanilla, I couldn't wait to see what he considered kinky. Looking up into his face, I found those sherry-colored eyes intently fixed on me.

"Good morning," I said, reaching up to place a kiss on his lips.

He hummed, sliding a hand up my back to tangle in my hair as he deepened the kiss. I pulled back, though his grip kept me from going very far.

"I have morning breath," I hissed.

The sleepy smirk he gave me melted my defenses, and he shrugged, lowering his face back to mine.

"I really don't give a fuck." And he kissed me again.

He stole my breath and warmed my body so quickly I scissored my legs, trying to relieve the ache. We were still naked, and I realized with no little amount of horror that my breath probably still smelled of his cum. My face felt like it was on fire as he moved away from my lips, biting his way down my neck.

"We should probably go have a shower," I hedged, groaning as he bit down hard on the juncture between my neck and shoulder.

He soothed the skin with soft strokes of his tongue before moving to my breasts to repeat the process.

"We will," he murmured between bites. "I'm eating first, though."

I protested half-heartedly, gripping his hair as he scooped my legs over his shoulders.

"Look how wet you are for me, my dirty girl. Do you want me to tongue fuck you good morning? Maybe I should wake you up like this every day. I'll have you happily up before sunrise."

I groaned. The image of him climbing into my bed, of waking up to him using my body, made me tingle in ways that felt shameful.

"Avery. Look at me." Logan had paused, his face so close to my core I could feel his breath teasing over the heated flesh.

"There's no shame in kink, okay? We haven't discussed limits, we'll do it today, but nothing you tell me will make me think any less of you. We're all turned on by different things, and if we're lucky, we find a partner that has similar interests. Don't hide who you are from me."

I nodded, releasing a long breath. No hiding. Okay.

"We good?" he asked, refusing to break eye contact.

"Yeah, we're good."

He smirked, hitching my hips up closer to his mouth.

"Excellent. Because despite your embarrassment, this pussy looks good enough to eat."

I gasped, gripping his hair tightly as he thrust his tongue into my opening, rubbing his nose against my clit in circles that had me panting in seconds. I thought of how he'd worked my other hole last night and felt my body tighten, wishing he'd do it again. I'd never tried anal play before, but the sensation of his tongue probing the sensitive area had made me feel out of control. Frenzied in the best possible way.

I hoped it would be on the list he gave me. I couldn't imagine working up the courage to ask him for it, but if I ticked it on a list with other things to try...

God, I was pathetic. Maybe I wasn't cut out for this kind of a relationship if I couldn't even ask for something as simple as ass play.

Without warning, Logan nipped viciously at my clit, shocking me out of my funk.

"Whatever you're thinking about, let it go or I'll fuck you until you're too blissed out to think."

I bit my lip, tempted by the offer.

"Christ, Avery. Don't look at me like that. I'll get you off now, then we can get to that list and set some boundaries. If overstimulation is on your green light list, you'd best believe we'll revisit this conversation."

He lapped at my clit with hard strokes, pushing two, and then three fingers, inside me, stroking my g-spot until my vision went spotty and my body liquified. Afterward, he lifted me from the couch and carried me into the bathroom, sitting me on the toilet seat while he prepared the shower.

"Did you have any plans for today?" he asked, holding a hand underneath the stream of water to test the temperature.

"Seeing as I can't leave the house? No. Not really. I'm looking forward to reading through that list, though."

The grin he threw over his shoulder was just shy of boyish. It made him look more his age than I'd seen since we first met.

When the water was ready, he helped me move beneath the flow and pumped body wash into his hand.

"I can clean myself, you know."

"I know," he said, reaching out and running his hands over my neck and across my clavicle. With gentle strokes, he worked the soap into my front, and then back, stopping just above my ass.

"Lean back against the wall," he instructed, kneeling at my feet and taking one foot in hand.

Working the muscles in my foot with firm strokes, he moved up my calves and thighs before gently cleaning my pussy and ass. Arousal burned through me, but nothing came of it. Once he'd ensured I was clean, he wrapped me in a towel, jumped back in, and did a much faster job of cleaning himself, then switched the water off.

"Actually, there's one thing I wanted to ask."

Logan paused in wrapping his hips in a towel. "What's that, hen?"

God, why did that nickname do things to me? I needed to focus before I chickened out again. Chicken. I was damned if the name wasn't fitting after all.

"I want you to find my mother. See if she is the one who has been following us. It doesn't make sense, but after that phone call and what Damon found out…"

He wrapped his arms around me, pulling me into his body as a slight tremor started in my arms.

"Of course I will, hen. Come on now, let's get you fed, then I'll set up the computer to do some research."

"After you've printed the list, right?"

He squeezed me tight before turning me toward the bathroom door. "After I've printed the list. You might be doing some research of your own today."

"Infantilism," I whispered, placing a definitive cross mark against the kink.

The list Logan had given me had been enlightening, to say the least. Some had been hard passes—no judgement, just not my thing—but others had left me intrigued. There were kinks I knew immediately I wanted to try, but still others I'd have to clarify with Logan how they would work in our personal dynamic before I committed one way or the other.

It was a fun exploration.

But even as I worked, I couldn't help glancing at my father's office, where Logan had opted to set up shop researching my mother.

I still couldn't believe I'd heard her voice after all these years.

"Avery."

Sweeping my kink homework into a messy pile, I swiped the papers off the table and answered Logan's summons with a little more enthusiasm than I would have even twenty-four hours earlier. Admittedly, thinking of some of the kinks I'd ticked off had left me a little hot and bothered.

I paused in the office doorway, drinking in the sight of Logan, sans ball cap, sitting behind my father's desk. His sandy blond hair flopped over his furrowed brow as he tapped something metal against the desk. A key, I saw as I closed the distance between us.

"What's that for?" I asked.

He looked up, face softening before he glanced at his tapping hand. "Oh, I don't know. I found it on the floor. Hey, come and take a look at this, will you?"

I came around behind him and looked over the document he'd been reading.

"That's my mother," I said, pointing at a DMV photo as he scrolled past it.

"Yeah, it's supposed to be. All of this is supposed to be current information on her."

I glanced at the side of his face, noticing the scowl had returned with a vengeance. "Why do you keep saying 'supposed to be'?"

"Here's the thing. This information was updated in the last couple of weeks. But this photo? She looked too young for her assigned age. I did a reverse image search, and the metadata on the image is from ten years ago. That's not the only thing. There are a ton of inconsistencies and missing information in the file. It's like someone has tried to backdate years of this woman's life. You're certain it was her voice you heard on the phone yesterday?"

"I mean... yes? I think?" Staring into the eyes of a mother I'd secretly missed as much as I'd resented her, I wasn't sure of anything anymore.

Logan hummed. "It doesn't make sense. Maybe I'll get one of my buddies to look into it." He turned, noticing the pile of papers in my hand.

"What do we have here?"

My face burned as I set down the list of sexual fantasies I'd compiled.

"Let's see..." He sat back, shuffling the papers into some kind of order.

"Blindfolds, biting, temperature play, bondage, worshipping, fellatio, spanking, flogging, breath play, choking, collars—fuck, you'd look good in a collar." He continued down the list, occasionally providing positive feedback, his wicked grin stretching wider the further down the list he went.

"Anilingus and anal play. I thought you enjoyed it last night. I think we're going to work well together. My only hard limit is threesomes. You're mine."

I nodded quickly, the note of possession in his voice sending goosebumps up my spine. He hadn't judged me for anything on the list, and the freedom I felt at having admitted those sexual fantasies was making me giddy.

Logan sighed, pulling me into his lap. "You are safe with me, hen. Always. There's nothing you can't tell me. This list makes me supremely happy because now I know how you want to be pleasured. Honestly, if you saw my own list, we are nearly a perfect match. In any scene we play out, you are in control. You know the safe word and have the ultimate decision on whether anything happens or not."

I believed every word he said, and for a moment, what should have warmed me to the core left me cold. Logan was here on my father's orders. Already, I relied on him too much, but I couldn't forget that as swiftly as he'd arrived, he'd be gone again after his 'mission' was done.

"And... she's back in her head. We'll have to fix that. Time to play, hen." Sliding the drawer beside him open, he fished out a charging cable, testing the strength of it between his hands.

"Wrists."

I held my hands out and watched quietly as he looped the cable around my wrists, just tight enough that movement was restrained.

"I don't want to go too tight with this. The last thing we want is to hurt you because of unreliable equipment. Feel free to pretend it hurts, though." He winked at me, and I grinned back.

"Okay, Daddy."

Logan sighed. "Ready for a spanking already, huh? Such a brat." He shook his head, feigning disappointment, but the spark in his eyes told me he was already playing with me. "Over there, nose to the wall and hands over your head."

I assumed the position quickly, forcing my mind away from what-ifs to the far more delicious present question of *what next?*

Measured footsteps approached, thumping like a bass drum, counting time to who knew what.

"Keep your nose on the wall," he ordered, grasping my hips and nudging my feet out.

My wrists slid down the wall a little, and he adjusted me so that my upper body pressed into the wall, with my back bowed and my ass sticking out. The position made it a little difficult to breathe with how my face pressed into the wall. Logan slid my panties to my ankles and coaxed my feet out of them one by one, encouraging me to take a wider stance.

"Beautiful." He checked the restraints on my wrists hadn't tightened and slid his hand down my arm, tracing the slope of my spine, then flipped my skirt up onto my lower back.

"Do you remember your safe words?" he asked.

"Yep, it's—"

"Don't say it unless you're using it, hen. I'm serious."

"Okay."

"Good girl." He ran his hand over my flank like he was petting a favorite animal.

I flushed, the words burrowing under my skin with little bursts of pleasure. I guessed he'd noticed the double ticks next to praise kink.

His hand disappeared, and I strained to see where he'd gone as his footsteps moved slowly away from me. There was a grunt and a crash, followed by, "Don't move." I hadn't even noticed I'd tensed, ready to turn around and help.

"What's going on?" I asked instead, settling back into position.

"I'm improvising."

I grinned, hearing the gentle brush of fabric as his footsteps came nearer. A cool, silky something creeped across my lower back. It felt almost like water. What was that? The sensation came again, an almost tickle as he ran the object over my shoulder blade, down my spine, and over my ass. It lifted away, and I braced myself for the tickle, trying to anticipate where it would fall next.

I sucked in a breath as it lashed across my hip in a stinging blow, followed by the soft tickling sensation soothing the skin. He repeated the action on the other side before working up my ribs, alternating stinging blows with gentle caresses until my skin felt hypersensitive. I anticipated the sting just as much as the soothing. More so.

"I'd ask if this is making you wet, hen, but I can see it dripping down your leg."

He was right. The sting on my skin didn't feel like enough anymore. I wanted it harder.

"Please," I begged, wanting him to take the hint.

"What are you asking for, hen? My hand? My tongue? Maybe my cock?"

Any of it. All of it. I just knew it wasn't enough.

"More," I said, unable to quantify what I was asking for.

The next blow came from underneath, lashing at my clit. I cried out. Logan hummed, running the soft fibers up my slit, getting it wet before he lashed out again.

The sting was sharper now.

"As you please, hen." Leaning over my body, he slipped the object down the wall in front of my face. A curtain tassel. Damn, the man was resourceful. It felt wicked using my father's upholstery for sexual games. The idea made me burn with arousal.

"We need to keep you quiet, hen. Open up." It wasn't easy from the position I was in, but he managed to wedge the soft cords into my mouth. They tasted like me.

"If you want to stop, stomp twice."

I nodded and was rewarded with a sweet kiss on the cheek before he pulled back.

"Now to address your continued insistence on calling me *Daddy*."

His hand crashed down across first one ass cheek, then the other. Yesterday, when he'd spanked me, I thought he had been hard. As his hand connected again, a yelp left me as the realization dawned: he hadn't been trying at all.

"Your ass looks so beautiful with my handprints on it, hen. Such a pretty shade of red."

I groaned as he changed his angle, fingertips grazing my labia with the next hit.

"Do you think I could make your entire ass red? You're taking your punishment so well, my good girl."

After a few more slaps, he stood back to admire his handiwork.

"Stunning." His hands soothed over my burning skin.

Unable to resist, I wriggled under his touch, desperate for more.

His hands moved to my wrists again, his fingers pressing into mine, checking for blood flow. He grunted, sliding a hand under my chest to pull me upright. With gentle movements, he unwound the cord and dropped it at our feet before pointing at one of my father's leather wingback chairs.

"Sit in the seat and hook your legs over the arms. I want you to open yourself up for me."

I groaned, realizing I still had the tassel in my mouth.

"Did I tell you to remove that?"

Crap. Leaving the thing in my mouth, I quickly moved to take up position. Cool air brushed against my core as I sat back in the chair. My face burned at the vulnerability of the position. Logan circled me, sitting on the small coffee table and hunching forward so he was eye level with me.

"I said, hold yourself open for me."

My legs twitched reflexively, wanting to close, to hide away from his watching eyes. At the same time, I felt the moisture building. With shaking hands, I spread my pussy open for him.

"Touch yourself, but don't go near your clit."

I nodded, shifting my grip to free a hand and started working my fingers over my labia, down to my entrance, circling through the mess of arousal I knew he could see, and back up, avoiding direct contact with the swollen bud that was begging for attention.

"Good girl. Now fuck yourself slowly with just one finger."

It wasn't enough. My inner muscles gripped at my middle finger as I slid it slowly in and out, begging for more friction than I could give. I mewled in frustration, keeping pace with Logan's instruction under his hungry gaze until I thought I would lose it completely.

"Are you enjoying exploring exhibitionism, hen?" he asked.

I huffed, half tempted to cry. I loved the way he looked at me, but the delayed gratification was grating. The whine that left my throat was heavy with all the pent up emotions I couldn't give voice to. He laughed.

"You know as well as I do that it was ticked on your list. Now stop pouting. Add a second finger and curl them up inside you. Look for the rough flesh just inside your entrance. Got it? Concentrate on that spot."

I shivered in delight as my nerve endings sang in response to the movement. Logan smirked and sat back, watching as my face mirrored the pleasure I was feeling.

"Good girl. Now you can touch your clit, Avery. Make yourself come for me."

Continuing the stroking, I moved my other hand to obey Logan's direction and barely made contact before a lightning shock of an orgasm ripped through me. Logan added his own fingers to my pussy, groaning as I pulsed around him.

"You're squeezing my fingers so tight, hen. Your pussy is made to be filled. You put on such a nice show for me, pet. I loved it." The words of praise fell from his lips, warming me up and extending the pleasure pulsing through me.

Eventually, I sagged back in the chair, boneless as I panted through the fabric in my mouth. Logan popped his fingers into his mouth, sucking my arousal off before he removed the tassel from between my teeth. Straightening my legs one at a time, he pulled my skirt down over my lap until I sat looking somewhat presentable once more.

"I don't know if I'll ever be able to step in here without blushing again," I said with a nervous giggle.

Logan smirked. "I've been hard all day, sitting in here thinking about what we did last time. I'm going to have to find a new workspace if I want to be at all productive."

I hummed in pleasure, sinking into the wingback chair and ignoring the wet spot beneath me.

Logan moved around the room, picking up the cord and tassel to replace. I wondered if you'd be able to tell what had been done with the tassel once it dried.

"Avery?" Logan's voice sounded odd.

I sat up, wondering why he was holding a painting in his hand.

"I knocked this down earlier. Do you know what this is?" The frame of the painting was thick, something that hadn't been obvious when it hung half hidden by the curtains. Halfway down the frame was a small keyhole.

"I don't know. Mystery painting? I asked, smirking at my joke.

Logan frowned and leaned the painting against the wall before turning to the desk.

"I think..." Grabbing the small key I'd seen him playing with earlier, he kneeled beside the frame and fit it to the lock.

14

LOGAN

*P*apers slid across the floor. Some documents bearing the seal of the US Army, and others handwritten notes and various correspondence.

"It looks like work things," Avery said hesitantly, toeing a loose sheet of paper closer to the others.

"None of this should be in a private residence, though. It's against protocol. Especially since your father has retired and moved into politics."

Maybe I shouldn't have looked into the frame at all. I started gathering the files together and froze as a familiar name jumped off the page at me.

Casualty: Lana Forster. Within expected parameters. Continue to phase two.

What the hell?

Avery shifted nervously beside me. She needed food and some aftercare. I'd pushed her hard. Curiosity could wait for later. Gathering all the loose sheets into a pile, I slid them into the bottom drawer of the desk and replaced the frame on the wall. Something suspicious was going on here —something beyond Avery's stalker—and I was going to find out what.

"Time to eat, hen," I announced, straightening and guiding her out of the study with a hand pressed to her back.

She glanced over her shoulder toward the desk at the doorway but didn't protest as we headed into the kitchen to find the meals Luciana had left us.

My mind churned over the glimpse I'd had of the documents in the General's study, obsessing to the point of distraction as I chewed my moussaka.

"I'm going to strip naked and run around the neighborhood to celebrate my newfound love of exhibitionism."

"What?" I snapped my head around to see her grinning wickedly at me.

"There you are. I was worried I'd need to start removing clothes to get your attention back."

"Sorry, hen. I was just thinking."

She hummed. "I know, but what can we really do about it? One mystery at a time might be a good way to go. At least those documents aren't going to get us killed."

I forced a laugh, worried that was exactly what they could do. She was right, though, finding the person who sabotaged her brakes and continued to lurk took precedence over documents that may or may not prove guilt of a crime already committed.

Hell, maybe I'd misread the situation, and the correspondence had meant something else entirely.

Gathering our plates, I washed them quickly in the sink and turned to see her frowning at the back patio.

"Did you go outside?" she asked, eyeing the open door. I hadn't, and my blood ran cold at the possible implications. Had we failed to close it properly last time we left the house? Or had someone taken advantage of our distraction and broken in?

"Any chance Luciana is still around, and we didn't hear her come through?"

Avery shook her head. "She left before I came in to see you. Almost caught me reading through the kink list. That is not a conversation I want to have with the closest thing I have to a mother figure."

I wanted to laugh at the look on her face, but my mind was already churning over risk and implications of the house being breached.

"We're going to move through the house. You are going to stay behind me. If we encounter anyone, you are going to run to my truck, drive to the farmhouse, then wait for instructions. Do you understand?"

Eyes wide, she nodded vigorously, complying with direction as we moved slowly through each level of the house. When we reached the attic, the room looked like a bloodbath. Bright red paint pooled on the floor, spatters decorating the walls in a macabre exhibition of Rorshchach images. The canvas beneath the window had been vandalized, the half-finished landscape marred by the words "Almost time" in a messy hand.

My stomach sank.

"They were here," Avery whispered from the doorway, her eyes fixed on the ruined artwork before her. "They were in my space." Her words came faster, aggression replacing the initial shock.

"We'll get it cleaned up. Let me check the perimeter first, then we'll fix it. I promise."

I swept the house on my way back toward the patio door, pausing to assess the entry point to find the lock scratched and evidence of forced entry. Checking every other access point on the ground floor, there was no further evidence of tampering, so I took my sweep outside and checked the perimeter. Two cameras had been disarmed in the same manner as the last time, creating a blind spot that had allowed the individual to avoid triggering the motion sensor alarms I'd rigged.

Damn, whoever this was, they were savvy. I had to get ahead of this person, like yesterday. Avery was counting on me, and I refused to let her down.

After re-engaging the lock and jury-rigging a lashing system to keep the door closed, I sought Avery out in the attic.

"Are you okay?"

On hands and knees, she scrubbed furiously at the paint stains the intruder had left on the floorboards.

"I want to find this fucker, and I want to stop them. No one invades my space to try to intimidate me. This isn't even about me! My father pissed someone off, and I'm paying the consequences."

She looked up, her eyes burning with an anger I hadn't seen in her before, and deeper, something I felt far less adept at dealing with.

"Avery—"

"Don't. I want—no, I need to be angry. Just let me be angry."

She returned to scrubbing, her shoulders curled in, knuckles white where she gripped the brush. A single tear fell on the back of her hand, and she wiped it on her shirt, quickly swiping at her face with a broken grunt.

"Look at me, hen," I said, inserting as much command into my tone as I dared.

I had dealt with men terrified of dying for years. Joking, needling, anything to distract them worked most of the time. Confronted by a woman I was developing feelings for? In the face of evidence that I might not be able to protect her? It was a struggle to keep my own composure, let alone provide comfort to her.

Avery's hands stilled. Instead of obeying, her head dropped until she almost completely folded in on herself.

"What if it is my mother?" Her voice was barely a whisper, but it traveled in the quiet room.

I sighed, closing the distance between us and sinking to the ground beside her.

"Then we deal with it."

"I'm not okay with you hurting my mother. I don't care what she's done."

She felt too far away for this conversation, or maybe it was because I couldn't get close enough, but I scooped her up and situated her in my lap, face to face with me.

"We don't know for sure this is your mother. You haven't seen her in a decade, and even if, after all this time, she did decide to make a play against your father, why come after you? We need more information, and I need to keep you safe while we find it. I want to go through the papers we found in your father's study. Will you help me?"

Avery pressed her forehead to mine as though absorbing my words. Her breathing evened out, and eventually she gave a small nod.

"You're right. Let's not jump to conclusions. There's a lot to my father that we don't know about, and I'd say it's time we learned."

THE FIRST TIME I SAW ACTION, I WAS IN THE FRONT passenger seat of a Humvee, driven by the General, back when he was a Colonel, waiting on the promotion to Brigadier General that came as a direct result of that day six weeks later. I had been sent to the drop zone nearest to camp under orders to collect our incoming OIC.

The second he had recognized me, he had informed me of his intention to drive, dismissing protocol and insisting he preferred to be in control. I remembered the awe I felt in the presence of a man who had dedicated his life to serve his country and achieved things I'd only dreamed of. We'd taken an unscheduled stop halfway to camp and come under fire from a nearby outcrop. The General had grabbed his service weapon and returned fire before disappearing in the rocky terrain. I remembered the terror of abandonment. My certainty that I wouldn't survive the hour.

Instead, I'd sat useless in the car while gunfire raged close by, and when the smoke cleared, the General had detained two of the enemy and intercepted vital correspondence that saw a shift in the tide of the war.

As we approached the imposing study doors, I felt as though I were back in that car. Knowing my life was going to be different in a matter of minutes. And not necessarily for the better. Avery squeezed my hand, and I tightened my fingers in return. This was for the best.

The papers were a jumble after having spilled over the floor, and after some strategizing, we decided the best thing would be to halve the pile and see what we found.

The first few pages looked to be bank statements. Money in, money out. Regular numbers that appeared to be his salary and expenditure. The fourth page began to show irregularities. An eight-million-dollar deposit was lodged without sender details. Alone, it wouldn't have invited my attention, except that the date of the deposit was familiar. I rubbed gingerly at the back of my head and wondered at the coincidence of the General receiving a significant sum of unaccounted for money on the day camp was raided and Lana was killed.

"Do you have anything over there?" I asked to distract myself from the freight train my thoughts had become. There was a fine, but definitive line between fact finding and conspiracy theorizing. I needed more proof than just numbers.

"Umm... photocopies of texts from a decade ago. Logan, I don't like this. Listen. *Target eliminated. She didn't fight. Ensure payment by twenty-three hundred hours.* Why does it sound like my father had someone killed?"

I shook my head. "We don't know what the target was. It could have been anything."

Avery hummed.

"There's a few more from the same number, more recent. The top is cut off, but whatever they said, he didn't take it well. *You know the price of failure to comply. Make your choice.* That sounds ominous." The smile she cast me was crooked and didn't come close to reaching her eyes.

"Hey. We don't know anything for sure. We're fact finding. Even if we do find anything, remember, you are not him. He is the only person responsible for his actions." She nodded and glanced back at her page. "Hey... whoops." She bent to retrieve the paper she had dropped as a loud crack preceded the almost simultaneous tinkle of glass and a thunk of a heavy impact on the far side of the room. Avery screamed, flattening herself on the carpet as I ducked behind the desk and crab walked around to her.

"Keep hidden. You're going to crawl to the door. Are you ready? Stay down. Go."

As soon as I confirmed Avery was clear, I moved over to the window and inspected the perfectly round hole in the glass. Cracks spider-webbed out from the entry point, but the pane had otherwise remained intact. Outside, there were no visible signs of life anywhere between the house and tree line from this angle. Granted, the shooter would have shifted as soon as they got the shot off, but they would likely stay nearby to confirm the kill.

Shit.

Either Avery's mother had received paramilitary training at some point, or the threat was an unknown entity. The paperwork certainly implied the General was in bed with some shady characters, but who was pissed enough to go after his daughter?

The only thing this afternoon had clarified for me was that the house had been compromised. We needed to move, and there was only one place I could think to go.

When I joined her in the hall, Avery put on a brave face, jumping to comply when I instructed her to pack a bag and ensure she kept clear of any windows or doors that could give away her position to anyone outside. I didn't miss the tremor in her shoulders as I hustled her out to my truck, or the glance she threw back at the mansion before we turned out of the drive.

"It's not forever. Just until the threat is neutralized. You'll be home in no time, I promise."

Avery squeezed my knee, interrupting the stream of platitudes I gave her as I scanned the road and nearby houses for signs we were under surveillance.

"I don't particularly care about the house. I just want this all to be over."

I nodded. Of course, she did. While I wasn't responsible for the threat against her, I sure as hell hadn't made things easy. In fact, I'd taken advantage of the situation, hadn't I? Shit. Talk about an unfair power dynamic.

"I'll make sure it is," I muttered, returning my attention to the empty street.

The sun disappeared behind the horizon as I crisscrossed the suburban streets, paranoid there may have been a tail on us. I went as far as to pull into the underground section of the parking lot at the mall, cutting laps before I chose an exit at random to evade any drone surveillance we may have picked up. Nothing seemed to be enough. When the prospect of jacking a car started to seem appealing, I hauled back on my protective instincts and decided we would have lost anyone who was following us by now.

Turning toward the highway, I headed for the one place no one knew about. Somewhere she could be safe.

The wheels of my truck rumbled along the asphalt, the hypnotic vibration comforting after the events of the day. I glanced across the seat at where Avery was curled against the passenger door. Knees to chest, she looked far younger than her years. Until she met your eyes. In those hazel depths, I could see every one of her twenty-five years and then some. I knew damn well she'd only shared parts of herself with me so far, but I hoped I could earn her trust, eventually.

"We'll be there soon," I said softly, interrupting the yawn stretching her mouth.

"Oh."

Maybe I should have taken her to a hotel instead. Shit, I could have at least given her the choice. I cleared my throat, intending to ask her opinion, when she dropped her feet to the ground and turned toward me.

"Do you think we could stay at your farm? I know it's not really move-in ready, but I feel safe there. Is that okay? I just can't face going back to the house any time soon."

"Yeah. Yeah, I think that's a great idea," I said, ignoring the urge to puff my chest with masculine pride. She felt safe in my run-down farmhouse. By extension, she felt safe with me. Hell yes.

At last, we turned onto the long drive that led to the house, and I watched in awe as Avery's shoulders dropped from around her ears. The frown that had marred her face softened as the building came into view, silhouetted against the backdrop of a sky full of stars and, just kissing the roofline, the full moon.

"I have some sleeping bags in the back of the truck. If you want to head straight inside, I'll bring in some supplies."

As soon as we rolled to a stop, Avery wasted no time complying with my orders. I almost missed the brat she'd been less than twenty-four hours ago.

Shaking my head, I crawled over the back seats and took stock of my supplies. I had a few old MRE's, left from God knew when tucked in the bottom of my equipment trunk. They would save us some trips into town until we came up with a better plan to keep Avery safe.

The sleeping bags were exactly where I left them, and beneath them was a bulk pack of candles. So we had lighting, bedding, and food sorted.

Hopping out of my truck, I carried everything inside, noting there were still two large drums of fresh water in the corner of the decimated kitchen. If I'd known we were going to have to stay here, I would have held off on the renovations.

Avery took the sleeping bags from my hands, disappearing down the hall toward the bedroom while I piled the rest of our supplies in the cleanest corner of the kitchen I could find.

"What are we going to do about this?" Avery's voice floated out of the hall. Following the sound, I found her staring bleakly at the bathroom.

"I'll prioritize it tomorrow, but in the meantime, if you need the toilet, you're going to have to dig a hole. There's toilet paper in the MRE pack."

She grunted, a cute little noise of displeasure that made a grin tug at my lips.

"Sorry, hen. Not exactly five-star accommodation, but no one knows about this place. You're safe here."

"I'm safe with you." The words were so quiet I didn't think they were meant for my ears, but the effect they had was profound.

I may have taken this job out of loyalty to her father, but circumstances had changed beyond anything I could have predicted. Avery had burrowed under my skin and become a part of me that I couldn't afford to lose.

Powerless to resist the pull she had over me, I dragged her body against mine and slammed my mouth down over hers. Stealing her breath and demanding she return the control she had unwittingly taken. I felt undone. The events of the day crashed over me, clouding my eyes with a red haze that wanted blood without knowing the target.

A dropped piece of paper.

That was the difference between a bullet in her brain and her standing in my arms right now. Warm. Alive. How the fuck was that possible?

I wanted to get closer to her. Wanted to bury myself so deeply inside that we coudn't tell where she ended and I began. As if I could protect her from the inside out.

"Logan." The word filled my mouth, plea and promise all wrapped in one. I drove my tongue deeper, eating at her, searching for her supplication.

A bite of pain at my scalp pulled me out of my obsessive pursuit as she tugged on my hair again.

"Logan, make me forget. Please. Use me."

Guilt curled in my gut. "Avery."

"Please."

15

AVERY

*L*ogan had been brooding for hours, and it didn't take a genius to guess he was blaming himself for the latest developments. The guilt was coming off him in waves of ridiculous self-flagellation, and I didn't know any other way to stop the thought process than to insist he do something that would distract us both. I couldn't take the distance he was putting between us, so I was going to reclaim that territory with my body, if necessary.

His scowl intensified for a moment, his eyes clouding in indecision, and I worried he'd gone too far. I didn't think I could handle him walking away again.

My heart pounded, the silence of the world outside making me feel as though I was hurtling through space, alone and terrified, in search of ground.

"Okay."

One simple word, and the relief squeezed my throat so hard I could only smile at him.

He still wanted me. Despite everything he was forced to put up with because of me.

No one had ever stuck by me like this before. My first boyfriend, the one who had taken my virginity in a coupling so embarrassingly short I wondered if it actually counted, had agreed to cut all contact within thirty minutes of meeting my father. Subsequent dates had played out in much the same manner. Girl friends had been out of the question for a while with my father's proclivities. I'd been achingly alone. Until Logan.

"Give me five minutes, then strip down and lie across the dining table." He pressed a chaste kiss to my mouth and turned back toward the kitchen without another word.

Chewing on my thumbnail, I paced the length of the hallway, my mind running amok with possibilities of what he could have planned. Despite his moodiness, or maybe because of it, I'd found his creativity in the bedroom quite thrilling, and even the thought of the list I'd marked up earlier for him had my ears burning with a combination of lust and shame.

It's all right to be open to experimenting sexually, I reminded myself.

"Time's up, hen," Logan called from the other room. The words shot through me, heating my core with the wicked undertone in his voice. The broody soldier had left the building. I was about to join Logan, the sexual Dominant who wanted to make me scream.

Hurriedly stripping out of my clothes, I strode into the kitchen, crawling up onto the hulking wooden table with a swing in my hips that I knew he was watching closely. A feral growl left him as I made a show of lying down and spreading my arms and legs wide, exposing and offering myself to him all at once.

"I'm starting to think you're trying to control this situation, hen."

I blinked up at him, trying to convey innocence even as I spread my knees a little wider, knowing damn well I was so aroused he'd be able to see me dripping onto the wood beneath me.

Circling the table, Logan reached my head and held his hands out for mine.

"Hold on to the edge of the table and don't move your hands unless I tell you."

"Yes, Daddy."

Logan cursed, and I couldn't quite suppress the smirk. He liked the name, even if he didn't want to like it. Plus, it was an easy way to be a brat and to make him punish me. He couldn't feel guilty about everything outside the room while getting creative with me at the same time. I hoped.

Logan ran his hand down my arm as he moved back toward my feet, his tickling touch lighting the nerve endings in my skin.

"I wanted to use ice on you, but that's going to have to wait for another day."

Glancing at the gutted remains of the kitchen, I had to agree nothing would be frozen in here any time soon. God, I hoped this thing lasted long enough to experiment with ice, though. The thought of the freezing cold sensation on heated skin, the way it would melt and drip off my body...

"I have another idea, though. Do you remember the words we discussed? Are you comfortable using them if it gets too intense?"

"I remember."

I doubted I'd need the words, Logan seemed to read me better than I could read myself when we were together, but the way he checked in and confirmed I was in charge gave me a sense of safety I'd never felt with a sexual partner before.

Logan picked up one of the candles he'd set up around the room for light and brought it to my side. Instinctively, my legs slid together, but he caught one ankle and encouraged me back into position.

"No hiding. We'll go slow, but I think you'll enjoy this. Remember when I asked to wax your pussy? This will give you an idea of how pleasurable it can be."

A part of my mind was dubious, especially as I watched a droplet of wax run down the candle and settle on his hand. He didn't flinch, even as more of the white substance melted and coated his skin.

Moving to my feet, he held the candle poised, waiting for my nod before he let a small drizzle coat my toes. I gasped, pinpricks of awareness rushing over my skin as the momentary sting warmed into something far more pleasant. He repeated the process on my other foot, then moved up to my thighs. Watching closely, he dripped the molten wax over my inner thighs, watching me closely as I absorbed the moment of pain before the rush of heat made me twitch with the need to squeeze my thighs together.

"More," I moaned, keen to feel the bite of pain again.

He moved up my body, dripping wax on each nipple, thick enough to make me bow off the table. Brushing the hardening substance away, he replaced it with his mouth, sucking and biting at my skin until it was purple. His breath alone enough to make me gasp.

The table was cool beneath my palms, the wood worn to a soft polish by years of use. I clung to it so tight my fingers cramped as he brought the candle to hover above my pussy and let a small amount of wax drizzle over my labia. I shouted at the sting and groaned as my sensitized skin tingled beneath it.

"Good girl," Logan muttered, picking the hardening wax away and kissing the reddened skin.

"Fuck, you look beautiful laid out like that. Do you like the candle? Want to keep playing with it?"

I nodded emphatically. I didn't care what he did to me, I just wanted to keep feeling. Stop thinking.

Logan smirked and blew out the flame, bringing the bottom of the pillar to my lips.

"Suck, hen. Get it wet."

I opened my mouth and ran my tongue over the hard length. It tasted vaguely like soap, but the base was thin and quite easy to take deep into my throat.

"Just like that. Fuck, hen. That mouth."

Putting the candle aside, Logan gripped me by the armpits and slid me to the end of the table, so my head hung over the edge at hip height. Unzipping his pants, he brought his tip to my lips, and I eagerly sucked him into my mouth, groaning as the salty taste of his precum hit my tongue.

"Bend your knees and drop them out to the side for me, hen. Nice and wide, now."

He gripped the back of my thighs, encouraging me wider as I nosed at his scrotum, enjoying the masculine scent of him.

"Good girl. I'm going to fuck you with this candle. If you need me to stop, knock twice on the table."

I groaned, understanding, enjoying the shiver it elicited from him. He was dominating my body, but I was still in control.

Logan shifted forward, burying his cock farther in my throat as something hard brushed over my clit. I lifted my hips, chasing the feeling as he worked his cock in and out of my throat in long strokes that gave me just enough time to breathe in between thrusts.

The candle moved over my clit again before circling my entrance and pushing in slowly. Though narrow, it was long, and once fully seated, Logan started pumping the candle in tandem with his hips.

"Fuck, hen. You feel so good. Your mouth is perfection."

I groaned, absorbing every word of praise as my body started to coil tighter.

Logan stretched his body over mine, blanketing me in his bulk in a way that could have been suffocating to someone else, but not to me. He sealed his mouth over my clit and sucked hard, pumping the candle into me with deliberate force.

"Come for me, hen. I need you to soak this. Come now."

Choking on his cock, I screamed as my release hit me. The lack of oxygen heightened the experience, my heart hammering as my lungs burned for air. I could have knocked, but I trusted Logan. As my head began to spin from a heavy dose of endorphins, Logan backed off, letting me suck in mouthfuls of air as my orgasm faded.

"Good girl. Take a minute. You did so well. Look at you."

I grinned, spittle running up my face as my head hung loose. After a few more moments, I locked eyes with him and opened my mouth, ready to take him again.

"Already? Jesus, hen. You undo me. You did so well. I'm going to reward you now."

He slid back into my mouth, and I closed my eyes, enjoying the slide of his velvety skin over my tongue. I loved sucking cock, but something about Logan's length comforted me more than anything I'd tasted before. Maybe it made me a freak, but Logan didn't seem to have a problem with it, so neither would I. For as long as this lasted, I'd take every chance I could get to suck him off.

Logan must have picked up the candle again. I felt the smooth length rub up and down my slit, dipping into my pussy before moving farther down. Sliding a hand beneath my hips, Logan lifted me, opening me up so he could press the tip of the candle to my back entrance.

"You have no idea how much I want to fuck you here. I'm going to buy some lube tomorrow so we can. For now, I'm going to use a candle to do it while I eat you until you scream for me again."

Pushing in slowly, he breached the first ring of muscle, and I groaned at the stretch. Folding over me again, Logan sucked and licked at my pussy as he continued to push the candle until it was all the way in. The stretch in my muscles sent small shivers through my body, and I lifted my hips, wanting more, wanting everything. Logan chuckled, lazily circling the candle inside me as he pushed two fingers into my pussy.

"Greedy little girl. You want more? Fuck, I can tell you like it. You're gripping my fingers so tight. Will you grip my cock the same way tomorrow?"

I groaned, nuzzling at his balls, wanting to take all of him.

"Such a good girl. I'm going to fuck your throat now. Remember, knock if it's too much."

I hummed, gripping the candle as he let loose, hooking two fingers inside me as he planted his other hand on the table and drove into me with barely restrained violence. I struggled to keep my mouth wide enough, my jaw aching as I tried to keep my teeth clear of his dick, but he didn't seem to mind. His focus was on where his fingers dipped in and out of me. My neck cramped, but the next second, he moved his free hand to cradle my head, adjusting the angle and relieving the pressure on my spine. His grip on me tightened, and then my mouth flooded with his cum. I swallowed again and again, but still it spilled from the corners, running into my ears and across my face as though he were marking me as his.

God, I wanted to be his.

His cock twitched once more, and he pulled out of my mouth, encouraging me onto hands and knees, facing away from him.

"You look so beautiful with this inside you. I'm going to have to buy you a proper plug to wear. Would you like that, hen?" he asked, tweaking the candle and making me shudder as my nerve endings danced.

"Yes, please," I said softly.

"Good girl."

Gripping the candle, he pumped it into me in the same long strokes as before, making me gasp in delight.

"You're going to come for me again, hen. Tell me what you need."

I groaned.

"Come on, hen. I want to hear you say it. Good girls get what they ask for."

Flushing so hard I wondered if Logan could see it in the candlelight, I murmured, "I want you to keep stretching my ass and eating my pussy. Make me hurt."

Logan made a choked sound and pulled the candle out. I hid my face. Shit, I'd gone too far.

"Eyes up, hen. Why are you hiding?"

"I'm a freak, aren't I?"

Logan tugged on my shoulder until I sat up, turning me to face him. Tears burned my eyes.

"You are perfect, hen. Perfect. I just wish I had more toys for us to play with. You deserve the world, and all I have to give you is this run-down house. Never hide from me. And never hesitate to tell me what you want. I'm going to give you exactly what you asked for. Okay?"

I nodded and moved back into position as Logan slapped my ass.

"That's for calling yourself a freak."

I giggled, wiggling my hips at him in invitation. Instead, he slicked his fingers over my slit, dipping into my pussy and pumping them slow and deep until they were soaked, then moved them up to my ass.

"Deep breath, hen."

I did as he said, breathing in and pushing back against him as he slid into me, scissoring his digits in a way that made my eyes cross.

"So tight. You're going to take my cock so well. But for now..."

Continuing to alternate between pumping in and out, and scissoring to stretch in all the right places, he buried his face in my pussy, using his teeth to nip and bite me into a frenzy until I couldn't contain it anymore.

My arms collapsed beneath me as my whole body turned to Jell-O. Shivers of pleasure cascaded over me, and all I could do was curl into a ball as they continued to work their way through me.

I hadn't known this kind of pleasure was possible before I met Logan. I just hoped I lived long enough to experience all that he had to offer.

"Logan," I mumbled, reaching for his hand. He kneeled beside the table, bringing his head close enough to mine that I could see every long, thick lash individually covering his sherry-colored eyes. Why did men always have such beautiful lashes?

"What's wrong, hen? Can I get you anything?"

"Promise you won't leave me? I don't think I'm strong enough to survive that."

He sighed, gently brushing my hair out of my face.

"You're one of the strongest people I know, hen, but I promise I'm not going anywhere."

16

LOGAN

*A*very passed out shortly after, right there on the table. I cleaned both of us up and carried her into the bedroom, where she had laid out the sleeping bags, side by side. Seeing her curled up there, so small under the covers, made my protective instincts roar.

This woman was mine. I had to keep her safe, no matter what.

I thought about the request she'd made before she passed out. How many times had she had to pick up the pieces after being walked out on? As great as the General had been with me, I knew for a fact he had never shown much affection to his daughter. Had he said farewell before he headed off on deployment? I'd never seen her on base, or at the airport waving him off.

Her mother was another story all together. I knew Avery was convinced her mother was the one after her, but instinct was screaming something else was going on. The information Damon had pulled up just didn't gel the way it

167

was meant to. Regardless of the General's political aspirations, someone didn't just turn up out of the blue to start targeting her own daughter to get at an ex-partner.

Despite the recent orgasm, I was antsy, unsettled by all the unknowns and a feeling I couldn't shake that the answers were right there, if I could just reach out and grab them.

Stomping out the front door, I settled carefully on the edge of the rotting deck and pulled Bear's number up on my cell.

"Hey, man." The phone had barely rung before Bear's deep voice was tickling my ear. It wouldn't have surprised me if he was waiting for my call. He'd always had a sixth sense about when one of the team needed him.

"Hey."

"What's up?" He kept his voice light, but concern still laced his words. Shit. May as well just put it out there.

"Too much without enough intel. We had to evac the General's house. We were compromised there. Bear, nothing adds up. The intel Damon gave us is full of holes, and Avery's convinced we're being hunted by a militant ghost. Fuck. I feel like I'm losing it here."

Bear sighed, the sound long and low in the way that told me he was sorting through not just what I said, but what I meant by it.

"Okay, I can't move past the militant ghost comment, so let's start there. What do you mean?"

I explained everything in detail. Avery's suspicions, the most recent attacks—including the bullet meant for her fucking head—and our subsequent evacuation.

"So you settled at that farmhouse of yours?" he asked, eventually.

"How do you know about this place?"

"I know everything." The grin in his voice was as annoying as it was comforting. I had backup if I needed it; and thank God for that.

We sat quietly for a moment, the evening breeze mussing my hair and reminding me that my ball cap was still in my truck. I rubbed absently at the scar on the back of my head, thinking of the other new information I'd learned, almost forgotten with the more pressing events of the day.

"Do you remember the night Lana died?"

"The night she was killed, you mean? Yeah. Of course I do."

I nodded, even though he couldn't see it. Bear had been furious at the attack, as though it were a personal affront that the enemy had infiltrated his camp and killed one of our own.

"What if... what if there were more to the attack than we knew?" I felt like a traitor even saying the words, and the silence echoed down the line was more cutting than any rebuke.

"Forget—"

"Tell me exactly what you think you know." Bear's voice was sharp as a whip, so unlike his usual laid back attitude that I pulled my cell from my ear to check who I had called.

"Logan." Softer now, closer to the voice I knew. "If you know something, man, you need to tell me. You know that attack never sat right with me, and while I wasn't as vocal as you were after the fact, believe me when I tell you I haven't stopped investigating."

Calling me vocal after the attack was like calling an amputation a paper cut. I'd been obsessed. The second I was out of my hospital bed, I was making enquiries, sending emails, harassing anyone I could reach to investigate the occurrence. We'd been in a heavily guarded location that should have been off the map to the enemy. We'd had assets stolen from under us, and the only casualties had been Lana, me, and five men on guard detail.

I'd run my career into the ground, making enemies of higher up officials with my refusal to let the mystery go. I'd never admit it to the General, but I left before they could kick me out.

"Logan."

"Sorry, just thinking."

I explained the paperwork Avery and I had found. The bank statements, the correspondence, and my suspicions, all of it. When I was finished, Bear let out a string of vicious curses that I would expect to come from Damon, not the giant teddy-bear of a man who acted like a mother hen to all of his brothers-in-arms.

When he had calmed down, Bear took a deep breath and released it on a sigh I felt deep in my bones. We were all tired. Tired of subterfuge, of fighting, or watching loved ones die. Tired of all of it.

"Okay. First thing's first. You're in love with the girl, aren't you?"

Every muscle in my body seized at the thought of that one word. Denial screamed through my head, thoughts overlapping, scampering over each other like rats fleeing a burning house. Too soon. Boss's daughter. Not a chance.

Fuck.

He was right.

I couldn't help but push out the denial, though.

Bear chuckled. "Trust me when I say I can hear your mind ticking over, and I know for a fact that's bullshit. I saw the way you looked at her after the car accident. You've been a goner for a while, which means I know you're going to fight me on this next thing.

"She's a distraction. You may think having feelings for her makes you the best man to protect her, but you know that's not true. Your attention is inside on her instead of outside on the threat. You need to be neutral on this one, buddy. If you can't be the objective third party, it might be time to assign someone else for the duty. There's a reason we weren't supposed to fuck around with others in the company when we were deployed."

I grunted. Why had I called this prick again?

Bear chuckled. "I can hear you thinking from here, and fuck you for insulting me in whatever way you just did. Just promise me you'll think about it, yeah?"

I sighed, groping for a packet of cigarettes I hadn't smoked in a long time. Damn, I could have used a smoke.

"Sure. I'll think about it. Not right now, though. Tell me what's going on with you? Distract me from my clusterfuck of a life."

A rabbit darted across the drive and under my truck's front wheel a moment before an owl swooped past on silent wings. The night critters chittered and scurried around the nearby trees, and I breathed the first deep breath I'd allowed myself all day. Bear murmured something, his mouthpiece scratching like he had covered it to converse with someone in the room with him.

"Is someone else listening to our conversation?"

I knew Bear was trustworthy, but if someone else had heard what we'd discussed...

"Nah, man. Of course not. I stopped by to see Charlie tonight, and she was just asking if I wanted a beer. She's gone back inside now."

The name of Adrien's widow turned the blood cold in my veins. I'd been so wrapped up in my own shit I hadn't even bothered to check in on her. And didn't that make me a shitty friend?

"How is she?"

"Charlie? She's good. Well... she's better than she was. Trying to move on and learn to live without Adrien. Money's been a little tight for her, so I've been helping out some. Fixing the house up and stuff. I don't think Damon's been able to face her yet."

Talk about a reality check.

The lesson I should have learned with Lana had been reinforced with Adrien. You could lose people in an instant. Instead of fucking around with Avery, I should have been working on eliminating the threat. Going on the offensive was the only option.

Decision made, I surged to my feet, only to realize it was late in the evening and any action plan would have to wait at least until first light.

"...come along."

"Sorry, what?" I asked, realizing Bear had been engaged in a one-sided discussion while I brooded.

"The baseball match for suicide awareness we played tonight. It's a shame you couldn't come along. It was wild. Smouch ended up with a black eye, and Jones broke a finger. The other team looked worse, though. It was the most full-contact game of baseball I've ever seen. Even the mascots got into it. We're looking at making it an annual thing. Bringing the other services into it. The paramedics who attended were interested in joining in next year."

I chuckled. "Did they want to play? Or be on hand to fix injuries in a more timely fashion?"

Bear hummed as though thinking through his answer. "Nah, they want to play... except for the one who rolled his ankle tripping over home base. I don't think he was much of a sportsman. We're talking about doing a friendly match in a few weeks. You should come."

A nearby thump caught my attention, and I moved around the house as I said my goodbyes to Bear, promising to think about the upcoming match.

"Sounds great, man. I'll talk to you later. Say hi to Charlie and give her a hug for me, will you?"

"Can do. And think about what I said, yeah? If you're too close, you won't get the perspective you need to get shit done."

"I know. Thanks for the chat, man."

As I lowered my arm, a stinging pain registered in my neck, and a tingling numbness spread across my jaw and down over my chest. An arm wrapped around my body, taking the weight as my legs buckled, lowering me to the ground. My thoughts felt like molasses, slow and confused, as I squinted up at the dark figure above me.

Through the soup of my thoughts, one word emerged, giving me a surge of energy that allowed me to reach out toward my attacker before my eyes rolled back, blackness closing in from all angles.

Avery.

17

AVERY

I woke to the sound of Logan's voice drifting through the open window. His tone was light as he talked about what sounded like a baseball game. He sounded less stressed than he had been earlier, and I felt my own anxieties lessen, knowing he was okay. It had been one hell of a day. I relaxed into the softness of the nest I had made for myself, surprisingly comfortable despite my position on the floorboards.

Sleep was pulling me under when I heard a soft clatter, followed by a scuffling that made my heart freeze. Knowing better than to call out, I slipped out of my sleeping bag and eased up toward the window. Outside, the light of the full moon showed a suspiciously human shaped lump lying in the dirt.

My breath caught. Was that Logan? More importantly, was he alive?

Adrenaline dumped into my body, making my hands shake and my legs cramp as the fight-or-flight response tried to take over. Breathing deeply through my nose, I reminded myself I would fight if and when I needed to. For now, I needed my wits about me. There was no sign of the attacker through the window, and as much as I wanted to run straight out to Logan, I knew he wasn't the target. I was. He could have been taken out to lure me, or to avoid him interfering with whatever this person had in mind. Either way, I refused to play their game.

Moving as quietly as I could, I slipped out of the bedroom and hurried down the hall toward the kitchen. I needed room to move. Room to fight.

The wooden boards on the porch squeaked loudly, and I froze, straining my ears for the next footstep. When it came a moment later, I sent up a quiet prayer of thanks that the run-down state of the house was working in my favor. Moving as lightly as I could, I eased across the kitchen and slipped out the back door into the garden.

A cool breeze brought the scent of fresh dirt and grass to my nose as I moved in a crouch along the shadowed wall of the house. A slight hint of diesel was also present. Had this person brought a car with them? Or was I smelling Logan's truck?

Shit, Logan.

I couldn't leave him here in God knew what condition, but getting caught by whoever this was wouldn't serve anyone either. I scrubbed at my face, indecision rooting me to the spot as I considered my options.

The subtle roll of rocks underfoot alerted me to the threat. Straightening, I turned as a fist glanced painfully off my left shoulder. Damn it. Distraction could get me killed.

The figure before me was dressed in black. A long-sleeved shirt strained over a heavily muscled build, cargo pants riding low on their hips. Their features were covered by a black ski mask, and I wished for daylight so I could at least see the bastard's eyes. I never forgot a person's eyes. Had my mother hired a goon to abduct me?

The next punch came at my face, heavy as a hammer, and my training kicked in.

Don't fight force with force. Master William's words whispered through my mind as I deflected the blow, aiming a punch at the ribs of the person in front of me. They were solid, and I rethought my game plan. Weak points. I'd never been particularly good at pressure points, though they worked a treat when I managed to find them, but there were other things I could do.

As the next punch came at me, I moved around it, grasping the wrist and pulling the arm straight before slamming my palm against the back of their shoulder. The ball came out of the socket with an audible pop, and my opponent let out a very masculine shout of pain.

Shoulder dislocations were a vicious, but easy maneuver when you were up against it.

The man swung with his other hand, catching me across the face in a stunning blow that made my ears ring. *Don't get hit, idiot.* I stepped inside the next swing, blocking the arm as I aimed a strike at the side of his throat. Soft flesh gave way beneath the blade of my hand, and I grimaced as I slid the hand behind his neck and brought his nose down on my knee. He drove forward, lifting me over his shoulder, and I shrieked. Without my feet on the ground, I couldn't gain any leverage.

"Shut up, bitch. Don't make this harder than it needs to be," he growled, squeezing my legs painfully.

"Why are you doing this?" I asked, not expecting a response.

"Because it has to be done." The words were dark. Completely self-assured. This wasn't someone who had been hired to help with a job, nor was it someone unstable. This person was completely confident in their actions.

He headed away from the road, toward the paddocks, and I wondered how far he planned on taking me. I hadn't seen another car, and surely Logan would have heard it approach.

Struggling to catch my breath, my eyes felt ready to pop from the blood running to my head, where I hung over his shoulder. Enough of this. I needed to get away. Forcing my body straight, I brought my elbow down on the base of his skull as hard as I could, following it up with a blow to the shoulder I'd dislocated earlier.

"Fucking bitch!"

I hit the dirt hard as he recoiled in pain, cursing as he lumbered toward me.

Crab crawling away from him, my wrist rolled as it encountered something smooth and flat in the dirt beneath my hand. A rock. Gripping it tight enough to feel the pulse in my hand, I waited until the man was looming over me. Waited as he leaned down. Waited as he gripped my other arm in a painful grip. As he pulled me to my feet, I twisted and brought the rock down on his temple as hard as I could manage. He crumpled beneath my hand, and I spun away, breathing heavily.

Not waiting for him to recover, I bolted back toward where I had seen Logan's body, praying he was all right with everything I had. Skidding on the dirt beside him, I checked his pulse and heaved a sigh as it thumped steadily under my fingers. Asleep then... or maybe drugged? I glanced over my shoulder but couldn't see any sign of my attacker. Had I knocked him out? No time to worry about it.

I slapped Logan's face, hoping for a response, an eye flutter, anything. The farmland, which had appeared peaceful only hours before, now seemed full of secrets. Eyes staring from dark corners, ready to consume me whole.

"Logan."

Tap, tap, tap.

"Logan."

His breathing deepened, brow furrowing slightly as consciousness finally returned. Choking on a sob, I scanned the night for any sign of threat before refocusing on my protector.

"Hey," I said gently, a tear dropping onto his face as his eyes fluttered open, irises looking black in the pale light of the moon.

"Hey," he said, voice full of gravel. "What happened?"

"I just kicked some guy's butt while you had a nap," I sassed, regretting it instantly as his face closed up.

"Hey, I was kidding. I'm pretty sure he drugged you. It was definitely a he. They were too big and punched way too hard to be female." I paused as that information sunk in. "I guess we're not dealing with my mom then, huh?"

I'd been so sure it was my mom. Had maybe hoped a little, because even though it would have meant she was trying to kill me, at least she'd have been close.

God, I really was pathetic. It seemed I had as many mommy issues as I had daddy issues.

"No, hen. I think you already knew it wasn't your mom."

I nodded glumly, offering a hand he refused to take to help him up. Instead, I got to watch him almost fall on his head twice as the drugs continued to work in his system.

"Damn arrogant bastard, you're going to fall and crack your head open because you can't stand to accept help from a woman."

"I won't crack my head. I have cat-like reflexes." As he said it, his body went on a tilt-a-whirl. I slid under his armpit to keep him from doing exactly as I had predicted.

"Sure you do, cat man. Come on, I don't think it's safe to stay here anymore. I don't know what happened to that guy."

The fact I was able to bundle him into the passenger seat of his truck told me more about the lasting effects of the drug than anything else.

Running into the house to collect his keys was like knowingly entering a minefield. I jumped at every noise and whipped around corners with arms up, ready to defend myself.

Once I was back in the truck, I wasted no time flooring the gas pedal and taking off into the night.

With nowhere else to go, I decided to pull into the parking lot of the twenty-four-hour diner in the closest town. It was somewhere familiar, and I'd noticed a ton of security cameras set up around the lot, probably to dissuade vandals, but it would hopefully work to discourage killers, too.

"Do you think coffee will help the effects of the drug wear off?" I asked hopefully, eyeing the cheery yellow light spilling out of the diner windows.

Logan snorted. "Coffee helps with everything. So do pancakes. Let's go inside. We can come up with a plan once we're full of caffeine and sugar."

I reached across the seat and squeezed his arm, happy to feel him warm and moving beside me. "I think that sounds like a great idea. Let's go."

Logan was still unsteady on his feet, so ignoring his grumbling protests, I ducked under his arm to steady him as we moved inside.

After situating ourselves in a booth at the back of the diner, out of sight of the room, but with a view of the front door, we ordered our caffeine and sweets and sat back, staring at each other across the expanse of the plastic tablecloth.

"How are you feeling?" I asked when the silence became painful.

"Like someone's taken a hammer to the back of my skull, actually."

I snorted. The unladylike sound escaping before I could cover it. It wasn't funny, but it occurred to me that the guy who had tried to take me would hopefully be feeling much the same way. It seemed only fair.

"Sorry. Sorry, that wasn't about you," I said quickly, hoping he wouldn't close the conversation down on me.

His red-brown eyes narrowed, looking brighter in the artificial light of the diner without the shadow of his cap to cover them. His hair was a dusty mess, disheveled in a way that was sexy, despite knowing how he had come to look that way. Leaning over across the table, I plucked a grass seed out of his fringe and fiddled with it nervously.

"You really fought the guy off?"

"Duh, I told you I know kung fu. I'm basically a badass bitch."

I hid my hands in my lap, hoping he didn't notice the trembling that told the full story. I had been terrified. Chi sao, sparring in the kwoon was nothing like the fight I'd just had. There had been no mutual respect between partners. No tapping out or do-overs if the technique wasn't right. I'd been fighting for my life, and if I hadn't known at a molecular level what to do from hours upon hours of drilling moves into my muscular memory, I wouldn't be here.

When I glance up from my lap, Logan's stare didn't waver.

"You are badass. It doesn't mean you should have had to be in that situation."

A waitress bustled over with a coffeepot in hand.

"Please," I begged, holding my cup out for her to fill.

She gave me a small smile as she poured and did a double take when she offered the pot to Logan. I couldn't blame her. Even mussed up, drugged, and in a bad mood, he was breath-takingly good looking. But more than that, he was smart. Loyal. And exceptionally good in the bedroom.

Despite the danger, and the fact we had been going at it like rabbits over the last few days, my body heated just thinking about what he had done to me on the table the night before. The way he cared for me after we played made everything feel so much more real. It made me feel like it was something that could be more permanent.

A vague memory floated through my mind, me asking him not to leave while I was blissed out on orgasms and endorphins. I should have felt embarrassed about making myself so vulnerable to him—I'd meant every word of what I'd said—but I didn't.

He deserved to know where I stood.

"What are you smiling about?" Logan asked, his lips quirking to match mine.

"Oh, just remembering all the naughty things you did to me last night."

Logan chuckled. "You were almost kidnapped an hour ago, and you're thinking about sex? A woman after my own heart."

I grinned, breaking eye contact to start fixing my coffee the way I liked it.

"I feel shit that I don't already know this, but do you have a job?"

I looked up in surprise. Logan rubbed the back of his neck, looking around the diner before bringing his attention back to me.

"It just occurred to me that I came into your life and ordered you around, knowing nothing about who you really were as a person. I know nothing about your life. Your aspirations, your goals? They're all a mystery to me. I'm ashamed to admit it, but I bought into your father's idea of you being an entitled brat, but the more I know of you, the less I believe what he's selling."

My mouth was hanging open. I needed to close it. Maybe say a word or two, but I was stunned. I'd spent all my life being underestimated. Ignored. I was a wallflower in my own home. A pretty ornament for people to look at and ignore, or worse, covet.

Logan saw through all that. He hadn't believed my spoiled rich girl act for very long, either. The scariest part of this whole thing was that I had the unerring belief that I could trust him.

"You know I teach the children's kung fu class at the kwoon. I get a small amount of money for that, but mostly, I have an online store where I sell my art. The pottery is generally the most popular, but I also do commissioned paintings. I was supposed to have a wall in an exhibition next month, but seeing as I may be dead by then..."

"Don't say that." Logan's face was fierce as he stared me down, as though he could keep me alive through sheer force of will. Hell, maybe he could, but I was tired. Tired of running. Tired of looking over my shoulder.

I sipped my coffee, looking out the window to avoid Logan's eyes.

"Where can we go from here? We're running out of places to hide," I said softly to my reflection.

Logan sighed, sitting back in his seat as the waitress returned, arms weighed down with plates full of pancakes and bacon.

"We'll figure something out. For now, let's eat."

LOGAN

*B*ear was right. I was far too close to be any use as her protector. The fact someone had got the jump on me. Had knocked me out, leaving her alone to defend herself? It was unforgivable. Thank God she knew how to fight, although thinking of any reason a well-off daughter of a General would feel the need to learn martial arts made me burn.

This was a woman who had learned she could only trust herself, and I'd reinforced that belief this morning. She wouldn't like what I had planned, but I wasn't seeing much other choice. I was going to have to hand her over to someone else while I tracked down the son of a bitch who put the bruises on her legs that she had tried to hide from me.

The coffee cleared my head enough that thoughts were coming easier as the minutes passed, and the night outside got darker. We had nowhere to go for the night, and the thought irked me more than it should have. Maybe in the morning I could ask Bear to take her in... although, he was spending his spare time helping Charlie. Damon, then. It would give him a little more purpose, and he already knew what was going on with the stalker. I'd update him as soon as the sun was up.

Across the table, Avery picked at her pancakes quietly, as lost in her head as I was in my own. I wondered what she thought of all of this. She hadn't asked to be involved, and from everything we'd uncovered, it seemed she had very little to do with the initial motivation. It all came back to the General. Even under artificial lighting, her almost-white hair glowed, like an angel sent to earth. Her long lashes rested on her cheeks as she avoided my eyes, and I had the urge to pull her across the table and make her look at me. Fix those pretty hazel eyes on me and see the truth. I'd failed her. I didn't deserve her, but I sure as hell didn't want to let her go.

"What are you thinking about?" she asked suddenly, brow furrowed. "You have a vicious look on your face, and I'm fairly certain you just scared the shit out of the waitress."

I glanced over my shoulder and noticed the young girl who had served our food scurrying away, sending wide eyed glances over her shoulder every couple of steps.

Shrugging, I reached across the table, drawing her hand to me and forcing her to lean in.

"I'm wondering how fast we would be kicked out if I bent you over this table and fucked you in front of the night shift. I'm sure they're all kinky shits who would get off on watching. What do you think, hen? Wanna put on a show?"

I was deflecting, of course, but the way she squirmed in her seat made my imagination run wild with possibilities. My dick hardened instantly, perking up as though he could smell her arousal from across the table, and I looked around, wondering how big the restrooms were in this place.

Beneath the table, something brushed against my thigh. Avery's foot. The wicked grin on her face turning her angelic appearance into something right out of a wet dream.

"I can't reach."

"You're insatiable," I said, shifting lower in my seat so she could press her foot into my groin.

Fuck, so was I. It wasn't the most comfortable position to be in. Her legs were so short I was almost under the table, but the pressure she exerted on my erection made it almost worth it. The fact we were in public and would probably be caught by the waitress any second, only made it hotter, and I could tell the thought had occurred to Avery too.

Her eyes darted from me to the door that led to the kitchen and back again as her breath left her in short pants. A beautiful pink flush crept up her cheeks as I palmed her foot and started working my hips under it, building myself right up to the edge before pulling back, drawing it out.

"Are you wet, hen?" I murmured, massaging the sole of her foot as I pulled myself back from the brink, enjoying the frustration at denying myself release.

"I'm pretty sure I've soaked through these shorts," she whispered back.

"Dip your fingers in and show me."

Her eyes widened and shot around the room again before she crept a hand to the waistband of her shorts.

I glanced around to make sure we wouldn't be interrupted and nodded at her to continue. The fact she complied without hesitation made my dick impossibly harder. This woman. Her pink lips parted, eyelashes fluttering as her hand moved inside her shorts for a moment before she pulled out glistening fingers.

That was all I could take.

Throwing cash on the table, I pulled Avery out of her seat and sucked her fingers into my mouth before pushing her out the emergency exit. In the darkness of the alley, I pushed her against the brick wall, kissing her hard, letting her taste herself on my lips. She groaned, rubbing herself against my erection as she met my tongue stroke for stroke.

I was gone for this woman. She owned me. And knowing that, the only thing that terrified me was the idea of losing her. I'd only barely survived Lana's death, and I hadn't felt even half what I did for this little spitfire.

"Get in the car. We need to go somewhere there aren't any cameras."

She opened hazy eyes, a tiny crease forming between her brows as she tried to fight through her arousal to understand my words.

"Okay," she said slowly, taking my hand as we headed toward my truck.

After I got Avery situated inside, I used the flashlight on my phone to check the undercarriage and tray of my truck for trackers. I deactivated the GPS on my dash and turned both

Avery's and my cell to flight mode before powering them down. Horny as I was, it hadn't escaped my notice that whoever was after us had known about my farmhouse.

Twenty minutes from the diner was a lookout I'd read about when I first bought the farmhouse and had never had the chance to explore. Now seemed like as good a time as any.

It took all my self-control to stick to the speed limit as we drove over dirt roads and through forest areas until we reached the spot. High above the farmland, hidden in the trees, it was a popular place to watch the sunrise during summer months. It was perfect. Secluded, quiet, and nowhere anyone would think to look for us.

I looked across the cab at Avery, who sat quietly chewing on her thumbnail.

"Are you okay, hen?" I asked, receiving a small smile in return.

She crawled across the seat toward me, straddling my lap. "I'm good, but I could be better."

Her eyes darkened as she raised her arms. I slid the t-shirt up to expose her tits, temporarily side-tracked as I took the opportunity to nip and suck at her soft flesh. She groaned, arching toward my mouth as she ground her hips into mine.

"Logan," she gasped as I bit down hard, soothing the ache with the flat of my tongue.

"What do you want, hen?" I asked, tugging the fabric of her shirt off her arms, exposing her flushed cheeks.

"You," she breathed.

"You'd better get these shorts off, then."

I slid my own pants to my knees as she rushed to comply. My erection sprung out, as ready as it had been in the diner almost half an hour before. I adjusted the seat back and held a hand out toward Avery.

"Come ride me, hen."

I helped her throw her knee over my hips and took a moment to appreciate her porcelain skin in the moonlight. Impatient for contact, Avery slapped my hands away and took my cock in hand, positioning me at her entrance and sliding onto me in one smooth movement. Our breaths left us in simultaneous sighs of relief as I bottomed out inside her.

She was so warm and wet, so eager to feel me stretching her. I brushed her hair back over her shoulder, palming her cheek as affection flooded me. At a loss for words, I pressed my lips to hers in a kiss I hoped could convey even half of what I felt for her, then did something I'd never done before.

Reclining my seat as far back as I could, I stretched my hands behind the headrest, clasping them tightly so I wouldn't be tempted to use them.

Avery froze, eyeing me carefully as she took in our positions.

"Use me, hen. I'm yours. Take what you want from me."

Her lips parted, breath stuttering as she watched me for another long minute.

"Go ahead. Just don't get used to it."

That got the smile I was looking for. She moved her hips, slowly at first, then with more confidence as she got used to the idea of being in control. She leaned over me, breasts swinging against my chest as she took a kiss. A quick, possessive claiming that made me grip my chair tighter to avoid spoiling the game. Straightening, she kneaded her breasts as she began to rock harder against me, using me just as I'd told her to. Sweat beaded on my forehead as the urge to come began to overwhelm my senses.

Not until Avery had had her fun. Her hand crept down over her stomach and paused, her eyes flying to me for a second, waiting for permission. I stared blankly back, silently reminding her this was her time. The smile she gave me was blinding, and I bit viciously at the inside of my cheek in an effort to maintain control as she began working her clit with two fingers. Her body tightened around me, and I knew she was close by the small whimpers breaking loose from her lips.

"Good girl," I whispered, unable to help myself. "Come for me."

She threw her head back, the scream that left her throat echoing through the cab of my truck and destroying the tight hold I had on my own orgasm. Wrapping an arm around her waist, I pulled her tight against me as shudders racked both of our bodies. Her breath blew warm over my neck where she had tucked her face close to me, her nose tracing my skin as she came down from her high.

"I love you." The words were so quiet, I could almost convince myself I hadn't heard them.

My stomach dropped. Buried inside her, sweat still cooling on our skin, I should have taken the confession as the gift it was, reciprocate because I was damn sure I loved her too, but I couldn't. Not yet.

Not when I planned to break a promise to her as soon as the sun rose.

We cleaned up as best we could and crawled into the backseat, curling around each other to grab a few hours' rest while we could.

THE SUN WAS WELL UP, DAPPLED LIGHT FILTERING through the trees onto Avery's sleeping head when I woke the next morning confused and disoriented. I'd slept without dreaming for the first time since... ever. I couldn't remember another time I'd slept through sunrise, and I wasn't sure whether to attribute the break in ritual to the residual drugs in my system, or the sex goddess beneath me. Detangling myself carefully from her limbs so I didn't disturb her, I slipped out of the truck and powered on my cell. Damon answered on the first ring.

"'Sup, man?" he asked, voice a little more nasal than usual.

"I got a favor to ask. Hey, are you okay? You sound off."

"Nah, man, just recovering. You know how it is."

Damn. I hoped to God he wasn't getting back on the alcohol train. He'd sounded better when he had been researching things for me, but maybe... then it hit me.

"Did you get messed up at the baseball game? Bear told me it was the event I shouldn't have missed."

Damon released a tight laugh. "Yeah, it was something all right."

My shoulders dropped. This was going to work. I trusted my brothers-in-arms more than anyone else in the world. If I knew Avery was safe, I'd be able to focus on finding her stalker and taking him out once and for all.

I explained the situation to Damon as succinctly as possible and waited through a tense silence as he thought it over. I didn't want to invade his privacy, but I quietly thought it might do him some good.

"Sure," he said. A chick, chick, followed by a deep inhale and exhale, came down the line. "Bring her around whenever you're ready. I'll make up the spare bed."

"I thought you gave up the smokes."

"Yeah, well. Crazy times, am I right?"

I couldn't have agreed more.

19

AVERY

"You can't be serious right now." I was going to explode.

My eyes burned with tears I refused to let fall as Logan stared at me, stone faced with his hand on the car door, waiting patiently for me to get out of his truck. So he could leave. Without me.

His buddy, whatever his name was, stood inside the doorway of what looked like a very nice little bungalow, silently watching our confrontation play out on his front lawn.

"Avery, please be reasonable—"

"Don't tell me to be reasonable, Logan. If you don't want the job anymore, just quit. I'll go home and protect myself. I've already proven I can do that."

I was tired, irritable, and breaking apart from the inside out. I knew damn well he'd heard me last night, and he'd said nothing. Worse than nothing, he'd immediately decided to hand me off to one of his buddies. Jaw tight, I breathed through the tightness in my throat and tried to swallow insults I knew I'd regret. But I wanted him to hurt. Why couldn't he feel a little of what was shredding my insides?

"Drive me home."

Reaching into the car, he grasped my jaw in a grip just this side of painful. "You are not going home until I know for sure this threat is neutralized. Hate me if you need to, but I will do anything in my power to make sure you are safe."

"Even if it means breaking my heart?" A tear slid free of my lashes, trailing over his thumb as I slammed my mouth closed. I didn't mean to be that vulnerable with him. I knew better than giving others the power to hurt me.

Logan's face dropped, his eyes softening into something closer to the man I'd seen last night, but the damage had been done. Pushing him out of the way, I jumped out of the truck, dashing my wrist across my eyes and striding across the lawn toward his friend. My steps faltered for a moment when I realized I'd met him before. The man from the mall. He gave me an understanding smile and moved back, making room for me to squeeze past him and into the house before Logan could catch up.

Stalling out in the kitchen, I sank into one of the stools that lined the small counter and tried to tune out the low buzz of male voices at the front door. A few minutes later, the guy—Damon, that was his name—strolled in.

"Logan said you might like a shower. I have some of Charlie's clothes here—you're about her size—if you'd like to put something clean on."

A shower sounded perfect. Trying to force a smile onto a face that just wanted to scowl, I thanked him for the offer and followed him to the bathroom where he passed me fresh clothing and a towel before leaving me alone.

I cranked on the water, stripping out of my filthy clothing, and surveyed the bruises that had formed after my fight the night before. How was this my life?

Without bothering to adjust the temperature much past scalding hot, I stepped into the stream, scorching my skin in hopes I could burn off the last twenty-four hours. Hell, burn off every minute since I'd opened the stupid envelope that had inadvertently brought Logan into my life. I'd known from the start he'd seen me as a job, but somewhere along the way, it had begun to feel like more. On my side, at least.

The body wash smelled like milk and honey, and I wondered if it was another thing Charlie had left around Damon's house. I couldn't imagine the brawny soldier using cleansing milk to keep his skin silky and soft when he showered. Slicking the bubbles over my skin, I intentionally wiped my mind of all thoughts of Logan, but I couldn't do anything about the ache he had left in me.

One day, when all of this was done, I'd take this emotion and put it into my art. I could create a collection about heartbreak and threats in the night. I could call it *The Target*. No, that sounded impersonal. Maybe I'd call it *Target Me*.

My skin was glowing a deep pink by the time I turned the shower off, towel drying my hair and body before I slipped into the clothes Damon had given me. I felt weird without any underwear, so I slipped my bra back on. My panties were stiff with a combination of my arousal and Logan's cum, so I rinsed them in the sink before tucking them into my pocket.

I stepped out of the bathroom feeling timid. I didn't know this man, and while I'd felt immediately comfortable with Logan, I'd been in my own space and convinced there were no monsters under my bed, just my paranoid father. Now I knew better. I found Damon lounging on the sofa, watching a football game on the television.

"Who's your team?" he asked, nodding at the screen.

I shrugged. I'd struggled even recognizing the sport. Even under threat of death, I couldn't have given him the name of a team, let alone one I liked.

"I'm more of an artsy kind of person," I said, taking a seat as far from the man as possible.

"That's right. You're more into martial arts, aren't you?"

I frowned, glancing over at him, but his eyes never left the game.

"How did you know that?"

"I think your father mentioned it."

"No, my father doesn't know I do martial arts."

Damon's eyes flicked to me, then away. He slapped his forehead. "No, it wasn't your father. I saw you leaving the kung fu place the other day, remember? When we ran into each other at the mall? Gold belt, that's pretty impressive. Have you been doing it long?"

I took a deep breath. Of course he'd seen me leaving the kwoon. I'd made him promise not to tell Logan he'd seen me that day. Paranoia was riding me hard today, and while I knew it was warranted, it didn't give me the right to be a suspicious bitch to Logan's friend, who had so kindly allowed himself to be dragged into this mess.

"Sorry, I'm not really myself today. I haven't even thanked you for taking me in."

He smiled, and I realized he was nice looking, even with the shiner. Logan had told me about the infamous baseball game, and at the time, had promised to take me to the next one. I wondered if he'd lied about that, too.

"Hey, it's okay. You're going through a lot at the moment, I get it. Just make yourself comfortable. Everything will work out."

This time, the smile I gave him was genuine. "Thanks, Damon. I don't know what possessed you to get involved with all of this mess, but I really appreciate it."

Damon grunted, glancing at the television before he pushed to his feet.

"Can I get you something to drink?"

"You got any vodka?" I joked.

"Yeah, I do. You want it in juice?"

I stared at him, trying to work out if he was pulling my leg. He shrugged, a naughty grin pulling at the edges of his mouth.

"It's five o'clock somewhere. What else are we going to do today?"

Logan had warned me that Damon had troubles with alcohol, but what would one drink hurt? Besides. Logan wasn't here, and Damon was right. We had nothing but time to kill.

Wandering into the kitchen, I tried to help Damon mix the drinks, but he quickly shooed me out. "I've got this. You go relax."

Maybe this wouldn't be so bad. I made myself comfortable in his recliner, curling my feet beneath me and perusing the various magazines on his side table. The most recent magazine was a *Sports Illustrated* from six months earlier, featuring some actor talking about his fitness routine for an upcoming movie.

Damon strode into the room a moment later with two orange drinks in hand.

"Bottoms up," he said, handing one to me as he sipped from the other glass.

The juice was cold and tangy, the vodka a dry bite on the inside of my mouth. Before I knew what I was doing, I'd swallowed the whole drink.

"Thirsty, huh?" Damon asked with a chuckle, pushing out of his chair.

"Here, I'll make you another."

"You haven't finished your drink yet," I protested, looking at the level of his glass. Damon flapped his hand at me. "What kind of host am I if I don't keep you well hydrated? My drink will keep. I'll be back in a moment."

True to his word, I'd barely read two sentences of an article on 'building guns that blast' before he was slipping a second glass into my hand. The first mouthful tasted a little different to the last glass, and I looked curiously at Damon.

"A little something extra. Do you like it?"

I smiled tightly and took a second sip, feeling my head swim.

"It tastes a little stronger than the last one," I said, leaning forward to place the glass on the table. I squeezed my eyes shut as the room span around me. The glass slipped from my fingers and exploded on the floor in a shower of liquid and glass.

"What...?" My knees hit the floor afterward, but the bite of glass cutting into my skin was a distant sensation as my hearing fuzzed out.

Damon placed his own drink on the table and stood calmly, watching over me as I listed sideways. It was hard to breathe, my whole body as immobile as if I'd been wrapped in plastic wrap. He bent down and rolled me onto my back, and I noticed too late something that made me scream and thrash inside my body which now felt like a prison.

He was favoring his right shoulder.

The one I'd dislocated the night before.

20

LOGAN

"*T*hanks for coming with me, man. I really appreciate the backup."

I felt like shit leaving Avery that way. I had a feeling there would be no coming back from that. I'd officially fucked up the best relationship I'd ever had, and I hadn't even had the balls to tell her how I felt. I had to make this worth it.

Bear grunted, pushing papers around. "I'm glad you called. I've been itching to go through this shit. Things just aren't adding up."

"Yeah, I feel you."

Bear glanced at me, deep blue eyes boring into my soul in a way I really didn't fucking need right now.

"You did the right thing, you know. Damon will keep her safe while we figure out what the fuck is going on."

"Yeah, I know. You didn't see her face, though. I fucked up. Bad."

"Did you tell her you love her?"

"No."

The look he gave me made me feel about two feet tall.

"You fucked up worse than bad, my man. Why the hell didn't you tell her how you feel?"

"Can we just make a start on this paperwork, please?" I muttered, moving around the desk.

"What's this? Rope play, temperature play, breath play... General, you kinky son of a bitch."

Fuck.

I snatched the list out of his hands, scanning the desk to see if there were any other pages lying around. Bear cackled so hard his eyes glistened with tears.

"Oh fuck, I would have paid to see the General's face if he'd found that list among his top-secret shit. Why the hell did you leave that in here?"

"We were being shot at, remember?" I pointed to the bullet hole in the wall, as though he may have forgotten the seriousness of the situation.

"Still funny," Bear asserted, chuckling as he looked back at the papers on the desk. "Okay, Sir, how do you want to sort this?"

I shot him a dead eyed stare. "Hilarious. Can we knock off the kink jokes now?"

"Yes, Daddy." He paused. "Oh, fuck, does she actually call you Daddy?"

Why did I like this guy again?

Instead of dignifying his comment with an answer—as if my flaming cheeks weren't answer enough—I resolutely picked up a piece of paper at random and started to read, ignoring Bear's continued levity at my expense. Once my idiot friend got over his case of the giggles, he sobered fast, moving through the papers as efficiently as I could do myself.

"Is this the correspondence you were talking about?" he asked, holding up the casualty report outlining Lana's death.

"Yeah," I said, barely able to read the words again.

Bear whistled through his teeth, reading over it carefully before putting it aside. We continued to work in silence until photocopies of a text exchange caught my attention.

The numbers listed at the top of the printout sparked a memory, and I scrambled through the papers until I found the text exchange where the General had threatened someone with the price of failure. The first part of the conversation was so much worse.

Collapsing into the General's chair, I looked back and forth between the pages. Bear looked up curiously and came around the table, slipping the pages out of my hands to read.

His ass hit the table with an audible thump, and we both sat quietly, lost in our own thoughts.

"He ordered a hit on me?" I said at last, the words shredding my throat as I forced them out.

The first part of the exchange was damning. It alluded to me getting too loud and ordered the recipient to take me out. Whoever was on the other end of the exchange refused, at which point the threat had been made about failure to comply.

Bear blinked, coming back from wherever his mind had gone with a curse as he pulled up his cell, scrolling furiously.

I knew he had found whatever he was looking for when the blood drained from his face. He snatched up the papers again, scanning the document before his eyes lost focus, his brow furrowed into a scowl that looked nothing like his usual cheerful self.

"We need to go," he said suddenly, pushing up from the desk and striding out of the room.

"What do you mean, we have to go? Where? Bear! Stop!"

"Avery's in danger."

That got me moving.

We slid into my truck, and I peeled out of the drive, hanging a left and then a right to head toward Damon's house.

"Talk to me. Now."

"Do you remember after the last deployment how Damon lost his cell on the last night? We were all convinced that the hooker he'd picked up had stolen it off him. He got a burner cell for about a month before he bothered to replace the old one. This was his number."

I glanced at the papers he shook at me before turning my attention back to the road.

"So... Damon was supposed to kill me? That seems really random, dude."

"No. It makes sense. After Adrien died, when Damon was drinking every day, he kept talking about shitty things catching up with him. He said he'd done things I couldn't even imagine. What if this was the shit he meant?"

"You sound like a conspiracy theorist."

"Do I? It's right here in black and white, dude. And if I'm right, we need to get to Avery right now. Fuck. If he's done something to her, it's all my fault."

"Calm down. You're freaking me out."

I threw the wheel hard to the left, taking the last corner into Damon's street much faster than I should have. We pulled up to the curb outside his house in a screech of tires and all but ran to the front door. Bear's panic was feeding my own, and as much as I didn't want to believe Damon was capable of the shit we'd been going through, I wasn't about to bet Avery's life on it.

The inside of the house was dark, and no one answered our knock on the door. They should have been here. Damon had said the plan was movies for the day. I picked my way through the garden and peered through the window into the sitting room. I could see a glass of juice on the coffee table, pieces of something glinting on the floor and...

"Blood." My heart leaped in my chest, trying to break loose and confirm for itself the blood didn't belong to my girl. My hen.

"Fuck this," Bear muttered, stomping back to the front door and smashing it with a powerful kick.

"Damon! Where the fuck are you?" he called, moving through the house.

"Clear," he called a moment later.

The world stopped rotating. For a fraction of a moment, I felt the earth fall away from my feet, and I spun through an infinite abyss. The grief I'd felt when I learned of Lana's death grasped my throat, squeezing tight enough to crush the life out of me.

A heavy blow landed on my cheek, knocking me out of my shock and very nearly off my feet.

"Get it together, man. Avery is not Lana. She hasn't been blown apart, and she sure as shit isn't dead yet. This is about the General. He'll want to gloat before he kills her."

Bear was right. We'd known from the start this was about the General. We could find out the details after we got Avery out safely. Wandering around to the back of the house, I noticed a green van parked on the grass.

"Shit. That van has been watching us for days. How did I not know it was Damon's?"

"He didn't want you to know. Come on. Isn't there a boat shed by the river down there? We went fishing out there last summer."

Breaking into a jog, Bear flanked me as we made our way over the grass and down to the riverside. A quarter mile downstream, we found the boathouse. The structure looked as though it had seen better days, the once cheery yellow paint curling away from rotting wooden walls. A large tree branch had fallen through the roof at one point, the gaping hole adding to the dilapidated look of the place.

Bear held up his hand, motioning me to approach on the near side while he moved around to the far side. I nodded, moving in at a crouch until I could look in through the window. Damon paced at the edge of the dock, hands gripping at his hair as he muttered to himself, a rambling stream of consciousness I couldn't follow.

At the edge of a worktable on the opposite wall sat a small handgun. Shifting to get a better look at the room, I stilled at the sight of Avery's unmoving form, slumped in a chair. Ropes held her small body in place, and the sight of blood running down her legs made my insides twist unpleasantly.

Movement behind Damon's back caught my eye, Bear moving into position. He glanced toward my hiding spot, counting down from three on his fingers. At one, he lunged for Damon while I sprang up and vaulted through the window.

"What the..." Damon wrenched around, crying out as Bear squeezed him tighter in a... Well... a bear hug. Much less pleasant than his normal hugs, though.

A pop echoed through the room, and Damon whimpered, falling still in Bear's arms.

"Was that your shoulder?" Bear asked in wonder.

"Fuck you."

Ignoring the exchange, I hustled over to Avery, lifting her head and checking her pupils, checking her pulse, and ensuring she could breathe. I loosened the restraints around her and laid her aside gently as Bear maneuvered Damon into her place. There was nothing gentle about the knots I tied to keep him secured. In fact, I took a sick amount of pleasure in his groans as I immobilized his bad arm.

"We want some answers, and I have a strange feeling you're the one who can give them," I started, straightening up and moving to stand shoulder to shoulder with Bear.

Looking down at this man whom we had fought beside, had been willing to die beside, I felt like I saw a stranger.

"We know the General issued a kill order for me, and you refused. Let's start there, shall we?"

Damon gritted his teeth, huffing great breaths through his nose, but between one moment and the next, the fight bled out of him. Before our eyes, he aged a decade, the pain in his eyes too real to be a farce.

"I was his killer," he said simply.

A small groan came from the body at my feet, and I dropped quickly to my knees to check on her.

"Welcome back, hen. It's okay. You're safe now." Avery's eyelids fluttered before flying open. Her hand lashed out, striking me on the jaw hard enough to turn my head.

"I deserved that, but come on now, hen. We're finally getting some answers."

As my voice registered with her, she relaxed, reaching a hand out to cling at the front of my shirt.

"It's Damon," she whispered urgently.

"We know. Look." I turned her head to show her where our former friend had been trussed up tight.

"Well, now that's sorted, back to this 'I'm a killer' thing," Bear said, taking control of the room.

"I was stupid. Broke and stupid when he approached me. Promised he could get me promoted faster than I ever dreamed. Adrien, too. All I had to do was eliminate one easy target and provide evidence." He scoffed. "You know the saying if the offer seems to be too good to be true, it probably is? Well, this was more like I put myself in a prison of my own making and took down the only person I ever loved with me."

I settled onto the ground, pulling Avery into my lap just to hold her close. I didn't want to think about what could have happened if we hadn't got here in time.

"The target was a woman. The profile he gave me said she was a threat to national security. I abducted her, recorded her last words, and disposed of the body where no one would find her." He glanced at Avery.

"For what it's worth, you were her last thought. Did you like the little recording? I'm sure she won't mind me laying blame on her, after all, she's been dead over a decade."

Avery recoiled as though his words could do physical damage.

"I didn't know I was acting on behalf of a jaded fucking husband. I got the promotion, chose whatever deployment I wanted, and in return, I occasionally got a tap on the shoulder. A little nudge in the direction of a new target. Adrien was so fucking happy. How the fuck could I have taken that away from him?" His eyes shone, pleading with us to understand his choices.

I couldn't keep the sneer from my face.

"And then you happened," he said, turning on me so suddenly that Avery hid her face in my neck.

"You couldn't let shit go. Had to go digging around where you shouldn't have. Such a good little soldier. It was the first time I refused a mission. I told him he could take everything away from me. Hell, give me a dishonorable discharge. I didn't care."

He laughed, the mirthless sound crawling through the space like a shadow extinguishing the light.

"The next day Adrien was dead. You put in your discharge, and he pulled the kill order. Everything wrapped up nicely for everyone. You get to live. The General gets to play politics and fuck up lives on a national scale. And what about me?!" He screamed the last words, spittle flying through the air as tears leaked down his cheeks.

"He doesn't get to walk away from this. He took my family, so I can take his. Don't you get it? This is justice."

It was madness. Unable to take any more, I stood, bringing Avery with me as we walked toward the door with an apologetic glance at Bear.

He nodded, turning back to our friend with a look of deep sadness on his face.

"Don't make him deal with it alone," Avery whispered. I realized her cheeks were as wet as Damon's had been. "He needs help." It took me longer than it should have to realize she was talking about Damon. She was right, of course. He needed psychiatric help, and fast.

Patting my hand, Avery pulled away from me and took a couple of stumbling steps back toward the house. When I tried to help, she batted my hands away, pointing resolutely back at the boathouse.

"Yell if you need me," I said, pinning her with a look that promised a lot of things I needed to say.

Bear was unwinding the ropes from around a sobbing Damon when I walked back in.

"That shoulder looks bad, man. You might need to get that seen to," I said, helping him stand.

"Yeah," Damon said, voice flat now that his story was out. We took a step toward the door behind Bear, pausing as he turned back toward us.

"No!"

Time slowed, Damon slipped out of my grip, growling as his shoulder tweaked and grabbed the handgun from the table. I whirled, throwing my hand out, but I was moving through molasses, and as tough as I was trained to be, nothing was faster than a speeding bullet. Superheroes didn't exist.

When a firearm is discharged in close proximity, hearing protection is always recommended to avoid damage to the ears. The thought, while appropriate due to the deafening blast that rattled my skull, was nonetheless unneeded as the back half of Damon's head exploded into the river behind him. The weapon slipped from between his teeth and hit the floor at the same time as his lifeless body.

"Logan!" Avery's scream echoed through the trees outside as Bear and I stood frozen, eyes fixed on our fallen comrade.

"Oh my God! Logan." Closer now, small arms wrapped around me, a golden head tucked under my chin, holding me up. Holding me together.

"Avery," I breathed, and it was a prayer I didn't deserve to have answered.

She squeezed me, waiting for my mind to clear the odd fog that had invaded it. My ears rang so loudly I could barely hear Bear as he crept forward, his shaking hands checking for a pulse despite the fact Damon's brain was probably already a couple of miles downriver.

"We need to get out of here," I said, my voice sounding foreign.

"We need to call nine one one," Avery said, fishing in my pocket for my cell. She was so smart. I had to tell her.

"I love you," I blurted. She paused mid-dial and stared at me.

"I'm going to pretend you didn't wait until after you'd saved me from a kidnapper and witnessed him blowing his brains out to tell me that. You get a redo. I want chocolate, sex, and absolutely no gray matter present when you do it. Understand?"

I nodded, unsure what else to do.

We waited on the riverbank for the emergency services to show up. Bear, Avery, and I stood in a shocked little line trying to figure out what the hell we could tell people.

It turned out we didn't have to.

The death was ruled a suicide. A soldier pushed too far who had developed an obsession with the General's daughter.

By the time we returned to Avery's house, once the authorities were done questioning us, the General was in residence, and his office was spotless. He thanked me for a job well done and escorted me out of the house with an exorbitant severance check.

"I told you there was money in personal security," he said with a wink.

"Actually, sir. There's something I need to talk to you about."

His face clouded into a dangerous expression I'd never seen before. I knew I didn't necessarily need to talk to him, but I hoped it would make Avery's life easier if we played nice. And ignorant.

"I'd like to ask Avery to move in with me. It looks like I'm the sucker willing to take your daughter off your hands." I felt sick saying the words, but the wry twist to his mouth told me he remembered our conversation from Adrien's funeral.

"Your funeral," he said, and I barely suppressed my gulp.

"Christ, I hope not."

The General chuckled nastily and tapped on the check in my hand.

"That isn't going to last you long, then. If I was going to trust anyone with her, it'd be you, son. Just make sure you keep in touch."

EPILOGUE

Avery

Six months later...

"Promise me the decking outside is the next thing on your list. I just got another splinter," I called as I pushed through the front door, arms laden with groceries.

Logan stood at the new kitchen counter, staring hard at a piece of paper.

"What's that?"

"They're opening an investigation into Lana's death. It seems some new information has come to light. They're implying it may also cover recent deaths of servicemen outside of active duty."

I dropped the bags at my feet and rushed over, scanning the letter in his hand.

"This is it," I breathed. "Do you think they're going to get him?"

He shrugged. "He has a lot of friends in high places. I never thought we'd get this far." Shaking his head, he deliberately placed the letter down, turning his full attention back to me.

"Get naked," he said, the command running through me like liquid fire, immediately dampening my panties as his mouth spread into a wicked grin.

Stripping out of my clothes, I crawled onto the counter, lying out on my back under his direction. He picked up a cup from beside the sink, and it wasn't until he tipped it up to drizzle a fine line of warm chocolate over my breasts that I realized he'd set me up.

"Chocolate," he said, running his tongue over my ribs, lapping up the sweetness in lazy lashes. "Tick."

He stepped back and dropped his shorts, then whipped his shirt over his head. In an act of athleticism I could only dream of, he leaped onto the counter, draping his body over mine, cock nestled between my legs so that as he moved, the head bumped up against my clit. Dropping his mouth to mine, he shared the rich taste of the treat in a deliciously dirty kiss.

"Sex?" he pulled his hips back and slid his cock into me in one smooth push. "Tick."

He held himself deep inside me, shifting his weight to dip a thumb into the chocolate, bringing it to my lips with a command: "Suck."

His thick digit tickled the back of my tongue, the combined stimulation making me twitch as he refused to move inside me. I huffed, lifting my hips in an attempt to tell him what I wanted.

Logan clucked his tongue. "Bad girl, hen. Are you trying to top from the bottom again?"

I whined, swiveling my hips in the hope he'd give me what I wanted.

"No. I think I'm quite happy here. Your beautiful, wet pussy warming my cock while you suck on my thumb. Should we change it up a bit?"

He removed his thumb with a pop, dipping two fingers deep into the chocolate and smearing them over my lips before I opened for him. I groaned at the combined sensations of being filled so nicely while the chocolate dripped down the back of my throat. Working my tongue between his fingers, I licked them clean. Sucking as hard as I liked to suck on other parts of his body.

Logan dropped his forehead to mine, breathing me in for a moment before he lifted completely off me. The only part of our bodies touching was where we were joined. He rocked smoothly, a rhythm that kept him from penetrating too deeply and made me squirm with the need for more.

"Am I being too mean to you, hen?" he asked, humor lacing his words with a playfulness that had become more apparent the longer we spent together.

"You're horrible, and I hate you," I said petulantly, crossing my arms over my chest.

He chuckled, dropping onto me, effectively trapping my arms between us.

"Well, that's too bad, because I love you, and I've decided you'll be my wife."

"Is that a proposal?" I asked, dropping out of the game in shock.

"That's doing my do-over properly, hen. You're mine, and I'm never letting you get away."

I grinned, arching into him as he began to move in earnest, knocking the chocolate to the floor as he drove me across the counter with the force of his thrusts. Logan pushed up to his knees, scooped me into his arms, and drove me onto his dick again and again until we were both sweating and groaning through our releases.

I didn't know what the future held, but I was glad Logan would be there to help me through it.

The End
Thanks for reading!

If you enjoyed **Target Me**, please consider leaving a review here.

While Logan and Avery's story is done, this series is just heating up!
Preorder **Heal Me**, Bear and Charlie's story, today.

www.tlhamiltonauthor.com

Sign up for TL's newsletter to find out about new books!

heal
me

at all costs series

TL HAMILTON

How do you heal when your life falls to pieces? When the answers you're given are lies?

Charlie Smith is a twenty-seven year old widow.

Rather than the blaze of glory her husband, Adrien, always spoke of, he passed in the night. By his own hand.

Supposedly.

Charlie doesn't believe it, and neither do his brothers in arms. Especially John "Bear" Grizzy.

While Bear works to uncover the truth behind Adrien's demise, Charlie is left to battle complicated emotions.

Grief.

Loss.

Desire.

Bear has a gravity that calls to Charlie in a way that feels illicit, and having him in her house is only making it harder to resist.

Solving the mystery may give Charlie peace of mind, but it could be that Bear is just what she needs to HEAL.

Preorder Today

ALSO BY TL HAMILTON

M/F Sports Romance

The Perfect Stroke

Split - Kane & Darcy Pt 1

Shatter - Kane & Darcy Pt 2

Shock - Evie & Xavier

Fox Academy

Kicking it with the Winger

Dark M/F Military

At All Costs

Target Me

Heal Me

Contemporary RH

The One For Us

The not so secret life of a wish maker

The not so secret life of a candy addict (coming soon)

Where in the world (Stand alone in 'The One For Us' universe)

Paranormal RH

Moon Dust Library/ Silver Springs Library Standalones

Moonlit Alexandrite

Moonlit Alexandrite: Crafty Seductions

Jewels Cafe: Jacinth

Anthologies

Hexes and Oh's (paranormal charity anthology)

ABOUT THE AUTHOR

TL Hamilton hails from Melbourne, Australia, where she lives with her hubby, two little boys, Arlo the wonder pup, and Hugo the turtle.

The consummate daydreamer, TL writes all over the romance spectrum from romcom right through to the dark, gritty hold onto your seats drama. Regardless of the story, you can guarantee you'll find relatable characters and steamy bedroom times between the covers of her books.

Reviews are the life blood of indie authors, so if you read her work and enjoy it, please consider leaving a review in exchange for her everlasting adoration.